*A
Harlequin
Romance*

OTHER
*Harlequin Romances*
by KATRINA BRITT

1393—HEALER OF HEARTS
1490—THE FABULOUS ISLAND
1525—THE UNKNOWN QUEST
1626—A SPRAY OF EDELWEISS
1679—THE GENTLE FLAME
1703—RELUCTANT VOYAGER
1727—STRANGE BEWILDERMENT
1760—THE GUARDED GATES

Many of these titles are available at your local bookseller,
or through the Harlequin Reader Service.

For a free catalogue listing all available Harlequin Romances,
send your name and address to:

HARLEQUIN READER SERVICE,
M.P.O. Box 707, Niagara Falls, N.Y. 14302
Canadian address: Stratford, Ontario, Canada.

or use order coupon at back of book.

# THE KING OF SPADES

by

## KATRINA BRITT

HARLEQUIN BOOKS     TORONTO
WINNIPEG

Original hard cover edition published in 1974
by Mills & Boon Limited.

© Katrina Britt 1974

SBN 373-01793-6

Harlequin edition published July 1974

Printed in Canada

1793

# CHAPTER ONE

From her lounger, Sara gazed dreamily at the smart cosmopolitan crowd around the swimming pool. There was music, laughter and romance in the air in this fabulous hotel, which had everything to offer from sauna baths to an exclusive night club. She had arrived the previous evening at Nice airport, enchanted by the silver carpet of moonbeams dancing on the still waters of the Mediterranean.

The airport bus had whisked her away past tall graceful palms, dark shadows of cypresses and a profusion of mimosa and bougainvillea neutral in the moonlight. Villefranche and Beaulieu, a tantalizing dazzle of lights against a dark velvet sky, had come and gone. Then, quite suddenly, they had been approaching Monte Carlo where the illuminated Royal Palace of Monaco perched above like a fairy castle. Down below lay the harbour where fabulous yachts bobbed up and down disdainfully with an air of hauteur among smaller craft. Sara, looking out on to the enchanting scene, had visibly relaxed.

Her rooms at the hotel were luxuriously cosy with her own bathroom, a balcony with a view and a phone beside her bed. Out-of-season prices had given Sara the opportunity to stay in one of Monte Carlo's most exclusive hotels with a fine view over the harbour. April with a promise of spring in the air combined with all the charm of a French resort was the kind of haven she welcomed after a grim English winter – a winter she wanted so much to forget.

Awakening to a blue and gold morning, Sara had breakfasted early and spent the morning exploring the tiny Principality of Monaco. After lunch she had written a few postcards, enjoyed a leisurely swim in the hotel's heated pool and was now reclining beside it on a lounger with a book.

It was the pretty girl in the scarlet swim suit poised

high on the diving board who cast the first shadow over the radiance of her day. She was so much like Maura, Sara thought unhappily. Thinking of Maura brought her thoughts to her own brother Julian. Was he forgetting his childhood sweetheart? Would he ever marry now he had lost her? Sara sincerely hoped so. He had been shattered when she had died. Sara sighed. Tragedy had no place in this happy informal gathering beneath the warm Mediterranean sun where no one appeared inclined to over-exert themselves. But Sara's thoughts, thus alerted, meandered unhappily on.

Sara and her brother Julian had known Maura Penhurst from childhood. They had grown up together in a rural district of Gloucester practically on horseback and had won between them a surfeit of trophies in that field for show-jumping. After training college, both girls had secured excellent posts in the French Embassy in London.

Julian lived in at the college where he lectured on nuclear physics and was only a short car run from the flat the two girls shared in London. Consequently, he was a regular visitor to their flat, and though he had never actually proposed to Maura, it was taken for granted that they would one day make a match of it.

The rift between them began when Maura volunteered to work at the French Embassy in Paris for three months. Her letters to Sara had been full of the good times she was having, quite innocent, so Sara believed, until Maura began to mention a certain fascinating Frenchman named Armand who also worked at the Embassy in Paris. Soon it was painfully clear to Sara that Maura was in love with him.

'Whatever you do promise you won't tell Julian about him,' she had written. 'He's the most fascinating man I've ever met. I simply must tell you about him.' There had been more to follow – parties at Armand's apartment in Paris, early morning rides on horseback in the Bois de Boulogne and runs in his fast car with a party of friends for moonlight bathing on some secluded beach.

Sara had read Maura's letters with her anxiety mounting for Julian. She was more than relieved when Maura's sojourn in Paris ended and she was to return to London. But Maura died the night before she was to leave Paris.

After her death, Julian, always lean and sparsely built, had grown haggard and pale. Eventually he had applied for and secured a post lecturing in a university in California. As his new appointment was not to start until May Sara had suggested him going with her to Monte Carlo for a holiday. But he had elected to leave for California as soon as his affairs were settled, and Sara, appalled at the change in him, had not tried to persuade him to go with her.

Apart from an announcement of her death and subsequent inquest in the press, there had been no scandal about Maura's untimely end. She had been in the habit of taking sleeping pills for insomnia and had taken them on the night in question after returning to her flat from a farewell party at the Embassy. Unfortunately, she had consumed a considerable amount of alcohol at the party and the sleeping pills had proved fatal. Accidental death, had been the verdict, but Sara had doubted it after receiving Maura's last letter which she knew by heart.

'I suppose you've guessed by now, Sara, that I'm hopelessly in love with Armand. I have been from our first meeting, when I found myself wishing that I had your looks. You more than anyone I know are the quintessence of the contemporary woman – lovely mouth, wide blue eyes, elfin face and lovely slender figure. What chance has an ordinary creature like me got of winning a man who is surrounded by chic beautiful Frenchwomen every day? In any case, he's hopelessly out of reach of yours truly. He belongs to the wealthy Romond de Poulain family who own vast estates in the chateau country just outside Paris. Oh, Sara, I want to die. I just can't leave him. I know you'll be shocked to hear this, but some day when you fall in love yourself you'll understand how I feel and not think too badly of me for what I've done.'

Unhappily, Sara roused herself from her thoughts and gazed across the swimming pool to a smart woman seated at a gay canopied table on the other side. She wore a gaily striped beach suit and a white coolie hat on her dark hair with an air of sophistication. Her long slender legs, beautifully tanned, narrowed down to narrow feet thrust into pretty multi-coloured sandals with laces twined around her slim ankles. She was a Parisienne without a doubt, Sara decided, watching the woman light a cigarette with the languid poise of a socialite. She was evidently waiting for someone and was suddenly smiling up into the face of a man who was strolling nonchalantly towards her.

Sara was instantly aware of everything about him. Tall, olive-skinned, black-haired, he wore his spare clean-cut look with an air of distinction. He had a wide intelligent brow and the obstinate jut of his masculine nose emphasized the clear, determined prominence of his jaw. Suddenly his mouth lifted into a charming beatific grin and he said something teasingly to the woman before lowering himself with a free masculine grace into the chair facing her at the table.

Sara felt strangely breathless at the man's kinetic magnetism and she could not take her eyes away from him. He wore expensive resort clothes with an indolent grace – fine linen slacks in beige, a superbly cut blazer in black with a silk maroon scarf at his brown throat. Casually he lighted a cigarette and turning to blow the smoke away from his companion, his eyes collided with Sara's across the pool. A deep flush crept up beneath her clear skin and she looked away hastily, annoyed with herself for being so rude as to stare at the man. He was a complete stranger, but she would never forget the startling impact of his black eyes – an impersonal gaze – a brief scrutiny, cool, but all the more disturbing because it had been so intent.

'Hello, Sara.'

She looked up, startled by the sound of the familiar rasping voice. There was no smile of welcome on her face for the ascetic-looking man in his late twenties who stood looking down at her grinning with a scarcely veiled triumph. For the second time that morning Sara was startled by the appearance of a man. This time it was one whom she detested.

8

'Stewart!' she exclaimed, taking in the bathing robe he wore over swimming trunks. 'I never expected to see you here. Are you with a party?'

'No. I came alone. Mind if I join you?'

He was already drawing up a chair and she watched him with barely concealed dismay. As he sat down the sun slanted across his fair hair, highlighting the brown eyes too closely set, the long nose and thin-lipped mouth. Sara had never liked Stewart Wilkes. It was a question whether anyone did at the Embassy where they both worked. He had a reputation of being a cold fish and tight-fisted too, according to Sara's colleagues, who usually gave him a wide berth. So far she had managed to do the same.

'Don't let me detain you,' she said stiffly, hating the way his eyes flickered over her slim figure as he sat down.

'I'm in no hurry,' he answered, by no means repelled by her cool reception. He had come to the same hotel as Sara with the object of improving their relationship. She had interested him from the day she had joined the Embassy staff with her expression of serenity and her concentration of the job in hand. He had known she was coming to Monte Carlo and it had been an easy matter to pump one of her friends to tell him the name of her hotel. He knew she did not care for him, but he was counting on her loneliness now that her brother had left the country. Since her friend had died she had clung to her brother Julian. Now he had gone.

She would be glad of his company soon, and he could wait. He stretched his legs out in front of him contentedly and narrowed a speculative glance at the mixed gathering around the pool.

'Quite a crowd,' he murmured. 'Half of them look as if they've never done a day's work in their lives.'

'How do you know?' Sara was stung to retort. How she hated his cynicism, his resentment against people better off than himself.

'You can tell them a mile off,' he went on as though Sara had not spoken. 'Take that woman in the white coolie hat and the handsome Romeo with her. I'll warrant they've never done a day's hard work between them.'

But Sara was already swinging her legs over the side of her lounger to the ground. 'Since you're so convinced, I suggest you make the lady's acquaintance. That way you can join the ranks of the idle rich whom you seem to envy so much.' She picked up her beach bag. 'So long, Stewart,' she said, rising to her feet. 'Good hunting!'

Without a backward glance, she marched back into the hotel where she was taken up in the lift to her room. What rotten luck to have to tolerate Stewart Wilkes! It had been bad enough putting up with him at the office and she did want to get away from it all. Disconsolately, she walked to the balcony to gaze out into the blue distance where the seagulls dipped and swooped in the sun. She would have given anything for the use of their wings in order to fly away into forgetfulness. Would the vague unhappy feeling of unrest prevalent since Maura's death and Julian's decision to leave the country ever go?

The trouble was that memories were as elusive as ghosts to pin down. One could not simply close a door against them. They filtered through, and the biggest of them was Maura. That girl in the scarlet swim suit at the swimming pool had been so much like her. Even the black-eyed stranger who had eyed her so dispassionately across the pool seemed to be connected in some way, perhaps because he was French. He had to be, with those Latin good looks and those brilliant black eyes. Stewart had called him a handsome Romeo. He certainly looked the part.

It was odd how she kept thinking about him – almost as if her brain had photographed him on her mind for all time. Like the memory of Maura. How absurd she was being, victimizing herself over the past. Maura had gone for ever. But Julian had only gone abroad. He had done right to break free of his past. In time he would look upon his affair with Maura as part of his growing up. Sara could find another job herself when she returned after her holiday. Why not? Brooding over the past was the right way to get morbid and self-centred. And she had never been that. She had to snap out of it. As for Stewart Wilkes, he was not important anyway.

Sara was down early for dinner that evening with the idea of avoiding Stewart. With her pale gold hair drawn up on top of her head into a small coronet and her gold tulle, full-skirted dress billowing out above the crimson carpet, she paused in the dining-room doorway. Her lips were tenderly curved into a bewitching smile when a waiter moved immediately to her side.

'A secluded table, Louis, please,' she whispered with all the aplomb of a celebrated star seeking seclusion.

'This way, madame.'

Louis guided her to a table partly screened by palms – an ideal spot, since it gave a full view of the room yet partly hid herself. Louis seated her.

'An aperitif, madame?' he asked politely.

'Yes, please,' she answered, noting with satisfaction that Stewart had not yet put in an appearance. He could not see her as he entered the room and it was doubtful whether he would see her at all since the tables immediately around her were gradually filling up. Louis had brought her drink and Sara was about to raise it to her lips when she was aware of a couple taking a table some distance from her own. It was the couple she had seen that afternoon at the swimming pool.

The man wore evening dress with an easy grace few could command. Looking mockingly amused and undeniably attractive, he was talking to his companion. Sara found him more disturbing than ever with the whiteness of his shirt front and cuffs contrasting sharply with his tanned skin. Something about him tormented her. It had begun with a faint warning tremor along her nerves when his black eyes had encountered her own across the swimming pool that afternoon.

The woman with him was obviously under his spell. Her svelte figure, in a dress of black and gold brocade, curved towards him and her face beneath the smooth black cap of hair was entirely absorbed in what he was saying. Suddenly they both dissolved into chuckles of laughter with the man's eyes twinkling roguishly, endearingly.

'Armand,' the woman cried, wiping tears of merriment from her eyes, 'you are ruining my make-up!'

The low husky voice came clearly across the room to hit Sara's ears like a gong. Armand, she had called him. The man was named Armand. Could it be? Surely not? It was too much of a coincidence. Why should it be Maura's Armand, the man who had treated her so disgracefully? Yet the woman could be a Parisienne, for her gown had the stamp of a famous fashion house. It was possible for them both to come from Paris. The woman wore a wedding ring. If they were a married couple then that ruled out the man, unless he had married recently.

Sara was trembling so much she had to lower her drink down on to the table. Her hand seemed to reach out of its own volition to touch the sleeve of Louis as he passed her table.

'Can you tell me the name of the couple sitting parallel with us across the room, Louis?' she whispered.

Louis cast a swift experienced glance at the couple in question. 'The lady is Madame Michelle Despard. The gentleman in Monsieur Armand Romond de Poulain.' Louis looked down at her untouched drink. 'The aperitif is to your liking, madame?'

Sara pulled herself together with an effort and managed a smile.

'Quite, thanks, Louis,' she said, adding, 'Not the same Monsieur Romond de Poulain who is attached to the Quai d'Orsay in Paris?'

'The same, madame.'

'Thank you, Louis.'

Sara wondered how she could remain so calm. That she could sit there casually sipping her drink with no outward sign of the upheaval within was something she would never understand. Yet there had been something about this Armand at their first encounter, a king of indefinable warning of danger forbidding closer contact. She had known it was not going to be easy for her to settle down after losing both Maura and Julian. It was only during the past few weeks that she had reached a kind of compromise with life by putting the past behind her and starting again. Now this sudden appearance of the man who was responsible for the upheaval in her life had brought it all back to her as if it was yesterday.

Sara could not remember her mother, who had died soon after she was born. After her mother's death, her father, a journalist, had spent most of his life abroad, leaving the staff of Everette House to look after Sara and her brother Julian, who was four years older than herself. She was sixteen when her father was killed during an uprising in a remote trouble spot in India, where he had been dispatched to report events. Everette House was sold and when Alan Everette's affairs had been settled, there had been enough money to send Sara to training college and to keep Julian on at university until he obtained his degree. The small annuity they had been left was mostly swallowed up for the stabling of their horses at Penhurst Towers, Maura's home.

Penhurst Towers had become a second home to Julian and Sara after their own home had been sold. But since Maura's death their visits had been marred by poignant memories. Major and Mrs. Penhurst had, however, derived a great deal of pleasure from their visits. Poor Major and Mrs. Penhurst, Sara thought. They had both aged considerably since the death of their beloved daughter.

Without being aware of it, Sara had emptied her glass. She placed it down on the table with a sigh, wishing she could forget the presence of the man across the room. She had expected that he would be attractive from the way he had bowled Maura over. It was easy to see how she had succumbed to his charms. That cynical mouth, for instance, held no sign of weakness. Rather was there a stubborn mastery about it – a kind of ruthlessness typical of the man himself. After Julian's brotherly approach, Maura had no doubt been thrilled by the technique of the handsome Frenchman. A fierce resentment kindled inside her. She could easily hate the man for what he had done to Maura.

The meal was excellent, although it slid down her

throat untasted. No one came to share her table and she was thankful to be left alone. Her presence did not go unnoticed. Absorbed in unhappy thought, Sara was unaware of several male glances in her direction. The air of serenity which outwardly she maintained added to her aura of mystery and charm.

At the end of the meal Sara went on to the terrace for coffee. With the exception of an elderly couple at the far end, it was deserted. Louis brought her coffee and she settled down into the white rattan chair upholstered gaily in blue and yellow. Above her head numerous fans sent down blasts of warm air to combat the evening chill of early spring. Beyond the terrace fountain sprays stirred a sweetness in the air of nocturnal scents from the immaculate grounds. Trees were laden with spring blossom and palms displayed their fringed foliage against a dark blue sky.

Sara finished her coffee and lighted a cigarette. At least she had evaded Stewart. But for how long? He had made no secret of his admiration of her at the Embassy, but she had never encouraged him. She moved uneasily, hoping he had not come to the same hotel with the intention of forcing his company upon her. She could think of nothing more nauseating.

The sound of the French window leading from the dining-room being opened caused her to cast an apprehensive glance in that direction. To her relief the slender form of a young woman appeared – the young woman who was so like Maura.

The newcomer evidently found nothing intimidating in Sara's wide-eyed regard, for she came forward eagerly, a poised young woman despite her youth. At close quarters she was not so much like Maura as Sara had thought. The thick unruly crop of brown hair and the brown eyes were the same, but not the classical nose and pointed chin. Maura's nose had been of the endearing button type generously sprinkled with freckles, her small chin square and determined. Maura had also been filled with lively animation with a constant flickering of laughter in the brown eyes.

This young woman was more serious and her clothes suggested an unlimited income. Her dress was stiff white organdie with a bodice of blue flowers. She wore a diamond and platinum watch on one slender wrist and exuded a delicate expensive perfume as she moved to where Sara was sitting.

'Miss Sara Everette?' she asked shyly.

'Yes,' Sara smiled.

The young woman bit her lip and went on with difficulty. 'I know you will think it odd for a perfect stranger to approach you with a request. I hope you don't mind.' She blushed with confusion. 'I saw your name in the hotel register. I also saw you at the swimming pool this afternoon.'

'I saw *you*,' Sara said. 'As a matter of fact you reminded me of a very dear friend – someone I lost.'

'Really?' Sara's words seemed to give her confidence. 'I would like to be your friend. May I join you?'

'By all means, if you wish.' Sara leaned forward to tap a long tube of ash from her cigarette into a nearby ashtray on a low table beside her. 'Surely you aren't staying alone at the hotel, a babe like you?'

The newcomer sat down gracefully and lifted a small militant chin. 'I am eighteen and, if I may say so, you don't look much older than that yourself.'

'I'm twenty-two. Do you usually take a holiday on your own?' Sara was not the inquisitive type, but this girl filled her with a vague uneasiness. She evidently came from a good family background and did not seem the sort of person to be allowed to roam about on her own. Something did not add up. But it was none of her business and Sara felt she had enough on her mind without becoming involved.

'No,' the girl faltered. 'I . . . I am here for a week. My name is Patrice Neilson and I wondered if you were going to the cabaret this evening.'

'Why ask me? Surely a male escort would be better?' Sara suggested.

'I . . . I don't know anyone here to take me. Do you?'

'I know one,' said Sara, thinking of Stewart. 'But he's

hardly your type.'

Patrice leaned forward eagerly. 'You mean the light-haired young man who sat beside you at the swimming pool?'

'Yes,' replied Sara warily, wondering what it was leading up to.

'I suppose you're going to the cabaret with him. I know this is awful cheek on my part, but I would like to go with someone. I wouldn't bother you if you would let me sit with you. I believe the cabaret is super and there's dancing afterwards. Does your friend dance?'

'As a matter of fact he's a good dancer. But would you mind telling me what this is all about?'

Patrice smiled rather sheepishly. 'Actually I came here several days ago with my grandfather after spending a holiday with him in London. I was to spend a week at this hotel with him before going back to my parents in Switzerland. Unfortunately, Grandfather was called back to London on urgent business.' Her brown eyes twinkled mischievously. 'He went with me to the airport in Nice to see me off, but his plane left before mine and he went without seeing me go.'

'And you didn't?'

'No. I came right back before they could let my room. I wanted a holiday without being attached to anyone. I only plan to stay the week. I shan't do anything silly.'

Sara eyed her calmly. 'You know it was very wrong of you to deceive your grandfather. He naturally feels responsible for you, and your thoughtless action could cause him unnecessary worry.'

Patrice regarded her just as calmly. 'I'm going home at the end of the week.'

'Suppose he has wired your parents to expect you? They'll be worried if you don't arrive on the plane.'

Patrice shook her head. 'Grandfather won't do that. He has too much on his mind at the moment, some big business deal, so he won't bother. Not yet, anyway, although he'll expect a letter from me thanking him for the holiday I spent with him.'

Sara smiled. 'I ought to pack you off home as quickly as

possible. Anyway, I'm glad you've approached me instead of some man.'

'But you don't want me butting in?'

'I didn't say so.' Sara looked at her levelly. 'In the first place I'm not going to the cabaret. In the second, you couldn't butt in on a situation which does not exist. My light-haired friend is no great friend of mine, merely a colleague who works in the same department as myself back home.' Sara was suddenly angry with herself for being moved by the girl's downcast expression. She wished she knew more about her, then was glad she did not. The holiday was becoming more unsettling than the life she had left behind. Besides, this girl Patrice reminded her too much of Maura, and she had come away to put the past behind her. Her next words came more or less against her will. 'However, I can sympathize with you seeking a little fun. It can't be very exciting taking a holiday with your grandfather. There are worse things . . . I can't see you having much fun with Stewart. On the other hand, you're quite safe with him, which is important. I . . .' Sara broke off suddenly as more people entered the terrace, including Stewart.

'So there you are, Sara,' he exclaimed, coming forward with a smirk of satisfaction on seeing her. 'I didn't see you in the dining-room. Where did you hide?'

He gave a curious look at Patrice, who looked quickly from one to the other.

But Sara was equal to the occasion. 'If it's a companion you want, Stewart, you have one right here. Miss Patrice Neilson – Stewart Wilkes.' She gave Stewart a bright smile. 'Miss Neilson wants to go to the cabaret this evening and she wants an escort.'

Stewart pulled up a chair. 'Really? This sounds interesting. Two lovely ladies to escort. This must be my day!'

But not mine, Sara thought wryly. She did feel brighter, though, since Stewart would be taken off her hands. 'I'm not going. It's entirely Miss Neilson's idea. I've told her we're colleagues in the same office. Miss Neilson is here for the week and she's at a loose end. She's looking forward to dancing after the cabaret, and I know you appreciate a good partner.'

Stewart's eyes glinted at her flintily. 'I take it you have an escort for the evening, my dear Sara.'

'No. I'm having an early night.'

Patrice said in a small voice, 'It will be all right, Mr. Wilkes, if you have other plans. You see, I thought Miss Everette would be going to the cabaret.'

'I have no other plans, and I've heard that the cabaret is very good. I shall be delighted to escort you, Miss Neilson,' Stewart said smoothly.

Watching them go, Sara was tempted to accompany them. She had put on an evening dress, but had not intended to dance in the ballroom or to visit the cabaret. Not tonight. She just was not in the mood for it. She had brought several good books with her and it would be pleasant to sit on her balcony and read for an hour or so before going to bed.

Full of her thoughts, Sara left the terrace via the French window which someone had left ajar and collided into someone coming out. Strong hands gripped her arms and a deep cultured voice with a faint accent spoke apologetically in her ear.

'I do beg your pardon. Did I hurt you?'

The question was so ludicrous coming from Armand Romond de Poulain that Sara had to take a firm hold of herself not to laugh hysterically. His eyes were really black with a devilish twinkle beneath the look of concern in their depths. Actually he had trodden on the top of her foot and she had drawn it back swiftly, stifling a cry of pain. She would have died rather than let him know.

'My fault as much as yours,' she said stiffly. 'And now, if you'll excuse me . . .'

Her tone and manner held a definite hint for him to release her. So potent was his effect upon her that she forgot the pain in her foot. The world shrunk in dimension to contain just the two of them, herself and this courteous man with the graceful manner and the white flashing smile.

There was a pleat between the straight black brows as

he retained his grip on her arms to wonder why her expression had frozen into a look of intense dislike.

'Are you sure you are not hurt, Miss . . .?'

The pause was a deliberate one – a way of seeking her name which Sara ignored. 'Perfectly,' she answered frigidly, wriggling from his hold. She knew she was acting out of character and being positively rude, but anger goaded her on. He stepped aside and she swept past him and stalked away. At least she tried to, until the pain at the top of her injured foot made each movement agony. She was limping when she crossed the hall to the lift and before she had gone halfway the Frenchman was barring her way.

'You are hurt, and I insist upon seeing you to your room,' he said curtly.

Black eyes warred with blue for electrical seconds. Suddenly breathless, Sara found herself meeting the merciless unswerving gaze, her anger overruled.

'You are behaving very foolishly.' His words were curt enough to restrain her from further resistance. He looked down at her foot and drew a swift intake of breath. '*Pauvre enfant!* Did I do that?' Sara followed his gaze and saw the mark on the top of her foot from his shoe. Amazingly, she thought, the damage was negligible, yet it stung like blazes. 'I am sorry,' he repeated, and without more ado swung her up into his arms and marched with her to the lift.

He carried her into her room and lowered her into a chair. Then he took off her slipper and strode into the bathroom to return with a towel part of which he had moistened with soap and water. His touch was so gentle as he cleaned the top of her foot that Sara hardly felt it. He dried the patch with the dry end of the towel and she saw a very slight graze beneath the thin covering of her stocking that still tingled.

'Hardly worth making a fuss about,' she said. 'I probably ricked my ankle when I drew my foot away so quickly when you trod on it. That was why I limped.'

His fingers moved around her ankle and he began a gentle massage. 'Can you feel it now?'

'A little, but it already feels easier.'

His sure touch and delicate perception were qualities she had not expected to find in such a man. He knelt looking up at her and again Sara was conscious of the same disturbing vitality in his gaze that she had felt when his eyes had met her own across the swimming pool. She was annoyed to find herself approving everything about him, even his voice with its male element and musical intonation which attracted her strangely. She realized vividly that his personal magnetism was undoubted, but it left her cold.

'How does it feel now?'

The massage had certainly eased the pain around her ankle. 'Fine now, thanks,' she gave him the briefest of smiles. 'I'll take a hot bath and apply a little antiseptic later to the graze.'

'Yes, do that. Sure you can feel no pain? You were walking badly just now to the lift.'

Sara shook her head. 'None. See, I can wriggle my toes.' She suited the action to the word. He watched closely, then eased off her other slipper before rising to his feet.

'I would now like to see you stand up and walk on it,' he said, holding out his hands.

Sara gave him the full benefit of wide blue eyes, feeling her anger mounting at his high-handedness. 'Is it necessary to make all this fuss? I would know if my foot was badly injured or not, surely?'

She spoke with a flush deepening in her cheeks to see he was in no way perturbed by her annoyance. He merely raised a brow, which made her put out her hands in an abrupt childish gesture and allow him to pull her to her feet. Sara walked around the room while he appraised her graceful, poised carriage.

'Satisfied?' she asked coldly.

'Shall we say relieved to see that you are none the worse for our painful encounter.' He drew out cigarettes from his pocket. 'Cigarette?'

'No, thanks.'

'Mind if I do?'

'No. But do not let me detain you. You have been more than kind and I have taken up enough of your time already.'

He was standing immediately above her, tall and disturbing, making her feel small and insignificant in her stockinged feet. She watched him light a cigarette with long brown fingers and wished he would go.

Memories stabbed like daggers as she watched him throw back his head and exhale the fragrant aroma of tobacco – Maura's letters – her tragic death and the subsequent unhappiness for all concerned. She wondered bitterly how he would react if she tackled him with it.

'May I introduce myself?' he said suavely. 'Armand Romond de Poulain.' His smile was one of extraordinary charm, but Sara refused to be impressed.

She inclined her head. 'Thanks for your help, monsieur. And now, if you will excuse me, I'm rather tired after a day spent in the invigorating air.'

Sara stiffened on seeing his smile of frank disbelief. 'But not too tired to tell me your name, I think.'

Her control began to slip a little. 'It need not concern you,' she replied coolly.

His handsome face assumed a pained expression. '*Touché!* I am concerned, very much so since I all but crushed your pretty little foot. I would be less than polite not to be concerned.'

'You have shown your concern, monsieur, and done all you could to help. Believe me, I'm very grateful.'

'But not grateful enough to tell me your name?'

Sara moistened dry lips. The man was used to dealing with women and intriguing situations, she thought, realizing that her very coolness could be encouraging him. Nervously, she began to wish she had not taken this holiday, which far from helping her to forget the past was only opening up old wounds instead of healing them. The hollows beneath her high cheekbones, accentuated by the past unhappy months, were more pronounced, giving her classical features a vulnerable look.

'My name is Sara Everette. I came here for a holiday and I intend to keep my own company.'

He digested this, blowing out another line of smoke ceilingwards.

'Are you not being rather selfish in keeping your own company when you can give others the pleasure of it?'

'This is a large hotel and I know no one here. No one will notice if I choose to keep to myself.'

'I would have noticed.'

'You would?' Sara held her breath. 'Why you particularly?'

'Because I would be curious as to why a charming young woman should wish to remain aloof.' The dark eyes were intent and probing. 'If you have been hurt emotionally surely the best way to recover is by joining in the free and easy atmosphere around you. It would have been much to your advantage had you left your troubles at the airport and collected them on your return journey. You would by then be in a fitter condition to deal with them.'

Sara listened with every scrap of colour leaving her face. How dared he? She clenched her hands, feeling sick and bruised with unhappiness which his presence increased a thousandfold. Angry words rose to her lips, but she repressed them, knowing they did not even speak the same language in the way of character.

Walking to the door with as much dignity as she could muster in her stockinged feet, Sara opened it to say quietly, 'Good night, monsieur, and thank you.'

For a moment he hesitated, the dark brows were raised mockingly. Then he bade her good night. It was some time before Sara's pulse went back to normal after he had gone. If only she need never meet him again!

# CHAPTER TWO

SARA's foot was much better the following morning. Strangely enough, after a most unsettling day she had enjoyed a good night and awakened refreshed and well able to tackle her problems. Her room was flooded in sunlight, making nonsense of her troubles. It was impossible to be in the least despondent in such lovely surroundings. After her cool reception of the amorous Armand Romond de Poulain it was unlikely that he would trouble her again. As for Stewart Wilkes, it should not be too difficult to avoid him while Patrice was there to take him out of her way.

All this went through her mind as she dressed, slipping on a pretty dress of buttercup yellow silk patterned with leaves. She had coiled her hair on top of her head and put white studs in her ears. She was treading into white buckskin shoes when a rap came on her door.

The pageboy who stood there gave a wide grin and presented her with a spray of roses with a courteous bow. Sara closed the door after him, her eyes riveted on the dark red velvet buds with the dew still fresh on them. There was a dozen in all, wrapped in cellophane and decorated with a pink satin ribbon. A card was attached, and with swiftly beating heart Sara read the masculine hand.

'I trust your foot is much better this morning. In view of the fact that it might be rather painful to walk on today, will you give me the pleasure of taking you out for a run in the car this afternoon? I shall be in the hotel foyer from two-thirty. Armand Romond de Poulain.'

Sara was staring at the firm handwriting with a mixture of anger and dismay when a second knock came on her door. It was Patrice, and she looked curiously at the flowers as Sara admitted her.

'I hope you don't mind me butting in on you like this,' Patrice said. 'I was on my way down to breakfast and I had to call in and thank you for last evening with Stewart. I thoroughly enjoyed it. I wish you'd come along. The show was super and I enjoyed dancing with Stewart afterwards . . .' She broke off as Sara handed her the flowers and stared in amazement. 'For me? Are you sure you don't want them? They're gorgeous and must have cost a packet.'

Sara shook her head with a faint smile and tore up the card into tiny pieces, ignoring Patrice's curious look as she dropped the fragments into a waste paper basket. She did not comment further, but she held Patrice's arm companionably when they went down to breakfast together after Patrice had taken the flowers to her room.

There was no sign of Armand or his companion when they entered the dining-room and they had finished breakfast and lingering over their coffee when Stewart joined them.

'I suggested to Patrice last evening that we all spend the day in Grasse. The weather seems to be favourable to a day outdoors,' he said, shaking out his table napkin after ordering his breakfast. 'Are you in favour, Sara? Patrice would like to go.'

He slanted a wary look at Sara, who was inwardly fuming at his nerve in being so presumptuous. She gave an over-bright smile and with a 'Bless you, my children' look said sweetly, 'I'm afraid I've already made my plans for the day, Stewart. But you and Patrice can go right ahead and enjoy yourselves.'

On her way to her room, Sara's feminine intuition told her that Stewart was angrier than he cared to admit at her refusal to accompany him. It was obvious that he was going to make himself a nuisance if she did not watch out. Thank heaven for the timely intervention of Patrice! A holiday with Stewart dogging her footsteps would have been the last straw, following all that had gone on before. Sara only hoped Patrice would not take him seriously. The man had not got it in him to make anyone happy.

A peep through her window at the stillness of the trees assured her there was no wind to speak of and, as Stewart had said, the cloudless blue sky gave a promise of a fine day. Acting on a sudden need to get away, she picked up the phone beside her bed and rang for a taxi. Then, repairing her make-up, Sara slipped a book into her handbag and picking up a white woolly cardigan went swiftly downstairs. A sudden twinge in her injured foot reminded her of the irrepressible Armand as she crossed the hotel foyer to find the taxi drawing up at the entrance. Yes, the taxi driver assured her, he knew of the very place, a secluded spot in the hills where she could sit in the sun and enjoy lunch at a restaurant nearby.

Within half an hour they had arrived. Sara alighted, asked the driver to collect her at five o'clock and looked around her with interest. Below her the road along which they had come wound like a ribbon through the hills. The vegetation around her was a lush green and apart from a group of young men carrying haversacks on their backs higher up on the summit outside the restaurant, she had the place to herself.

Sara strolled to a semi-circle of rocks sheltered but open to the full blast of the sun and sitting down took out her book. Later, after lunch at the restaurant, she returned to the nook among the rocks and gazed out dreamily on the panoramic view. Sunshine enhances the beauty of a place, but even a dull day could not take away the appeal of the lovely stretch of coastline with its rocky bays and sandy beaches. Sara drank in the beauty of it all with a sigh, ignoring the uneasy twinge at the thought of Armand Romond de Poulain waiting hopefully for her in the hotel foyer.

She could imagine him striding in expecting her to be late. He would lower his long length into a chair with a ful view of the lift, light a cigarette and pick up a newspaper with a relaxed air. Well, for once he was not having things his own way, and replete with a very satisfying lunch, Sara leaned back against the sun-warmed rock and closed her eyes.

Sara must have slept, for she was awakened by some sixth sense telling her she was not alone. Slowly, her blue eyes opened and her head turned almost of its own volition.

'Do not look so scared,' said Armand quietly by her side. 'You chose this outlandish spot to get away from me, and it is your own fault if you feel I have you at my mercy.' He chuckled at her wide-eyed look, finding it strangely childlike. 'You are looking at me as though I am a bogey man. It was very naughty of you to stand me up. Why not give a man a break and let him make up for the damage he has done to your pretty little foot? How is it, by the way?'

Looking down her slim legs appraisingly, he concentrated on her injured foot.

'Better,' she answered coldly. 'I should not be here if it wasn't.'

Her face grew hot as she wondered how long he had been reclining beside her. He lay at full length, turning her way and supported by a bent arm.

His lips twitched. 'You blush delightfully and are utterly transparent and sweet. I had no idea they made women like you nowadays.'

'Perhaps that's why you can't take a hint,' she retorted. 'If you wanted your revenge you certainly succeeded, for you half scared me out of my wits.'

'Guilty conscience,' he murmured, in no way abashed. 'I am sorry I scared you. I had no intention of doing so.'

'You're not sorry,' Sara argued. 'You're enjoying the situation. I'm not. Surely you can see that your presence is not welcome?'

'I am afraid you have no idea of the kind of man I am. I always complete any unfinished business. I heartily detest any loose ends and I always endeavour to tie them up neatly. Treading on your foot last evening awoke all my latent chivalry. I wanted to make amends for the pain I had caused you.' He drew a slim cigarette case from his pocket as he spoke. 'Cigarette?' She shook her head and he asked permission to smoke himself.

Sara looked at the strong dark face and the lean brown fingers manipulating the cigarette and lighter and waited. Presently he removed the cigarette from his lips to study the glowing end thoughtfully.

26

'Tell me about yourself. Is this your first visit to Monte Carlo?'

'Yes,' she answered laconically.

'Oh, come, you can do better than that. Why not relax?' He appeared relaxed himself, though his smile held a flickering fire. His arrogant confidence in his ability to charm froze Sara, who was wondering how on earth he had discovered her place of retreat.

'How did you know I was here?' she asked, refusing to budge an inch.

'Your taxi driver is an old friend of mine. He had a cab in Paris for years until he came here to Monte Carlo. A few discreet inquiries and here I am. Hard luck, you hiring his particular cab.'

'Yes, isn't it?'

He altered his position to look at her more fully. 'You have not forgiven me for treading on your foot, have you?'

Sara stiffened. He was being deliberately obtuse and she would have to put up with it until such time that he took his leave. She had only to freeze him off.

'I'm not angry with you for treading on my foot,' she insisted. 'It was an accident.'

He had put the cigarette to his lips and calmly blew out a line of smoke heavenwards. 'Then why refuse to go out with me this afternoon? I am perfectly respectable.'

'Because I don't choose to have people thrust upon me. I prefer to make my own friends.'

'You are fencing with me. You know as well as I that usually the most delightful incidents in life come from the unexpected encounter.' The black eyes narrowed between closing lids. 'I am trying to size you up.'

'Or cut me down to size,' she quipped.

He smiled. 'My first impression of you was that you were sweet and unspoilt with plenty of ideals and a wonderful sense of loyalty. Yet your behaviour towards me is boorish and rude. If you are attempting to scare me off, I do not scare easily.'

'Too bad,' she replied, her blue eyes flashing fire. 'Why the interest in me, monsieur? I'm certainly not interested in you.'

'*Touché,*' he said, still with that charming smile. 'Would you have me believe that had you hurt my foot you would not have bothered to inquire how I was faring?'

If only he knew, she would do more than graze his foot given the opportunity. Why should he get away with inadvertently causing Maura's death and all the misery to those concerned? But Sara was not the vindictive type, so the thought was only fleeting. It was then she remembered the roses. At least she had not forgotten her manners, if they were an unwelcome gift.

'The question does not arise, does it? I appreciate your help and I thank you for the roses. It was very kind of you. Now, I suggest we call it quits and that you leave me in peace.'

He gave a pained smile and said softly, 'You have a frozen heart, *chérie,* which one man some day is going to thaw. I will not accept you as an ice maiden – not with those eyes nor that mouth.' His smile was brilliantly audacious as his eyes lingered upon her mouth. 'I am of the opinion that someone should do something about it and take you in hand. Shall we begin with a car run to allow the scenery to soften you up a little? While the weather is warm the ground of these hills is still damp after the drop in night temperatures. It isn't wise to sit long. Come, I will not take no for an answer.' He was on his feet in one fluid movement and bending down with a twinkle in the dark eyes, offering his hands to help her to her feet.

Sara, making no effort to move, regarded him calmly. 'I will come on one condition,' she stipulated. 'That you leave me alone, don't seek me out or send me flowers.'

He hesitated, tongue in cheek. There was mastery in the burning ardent black eyes as he looked down at her with a fiery intensity. 'You drive a hard bargain. After all, I did not deliberately tread on your foot. An accident brought us together. Who knows, next time you will be falling into my arms happily?'

Sara's mouth grew suddenly firm. 'If you refuse to leave me alone I can always complain to the manager of the hotel.'

Calmly he reached for her hands and drew her up on her feet. 'I would not advise that if I were you. I am held in great esteem here as in Paris. Do you know what I shall do if you carry out your threat?' Little devils danced in the blackness of his eyes. 'I shall inform Monsieur that we have had a lovers' quarrel and that Mademoiselle is playing hard to get.'

Beneath the grip of his fingers, Sara felt a stab of fear prodding her into a new excitement. The air between them was charged with electric current flashing to and fro. She could not speak for the wild beating of her heart – all the neutral self-possession she had willed to the surface was swept away, leaving her with an adorable confusion and bewilderment deepening the blue of her eyes.

His expression changed to one of whimsical tenderness. He shook her gently.

'Why not capitulate and enjoy what the gods offer? You will only hurt yourself, never me. I usually get what I want.'

Sara's face was white and set. 'No,' she said, her eyes haunted.

'Why?' he asked with the arrogance of ultimate victory.

'Because I don't like you.'

'But you do not know me.'

'I have no wish to.'

He did not answer right away. He seemed to be considering the matter. He said finally, 'There, you have thrown down the gauntlet and it is for me to pick it up. In any case, you will have to accept a lift back in my car. I took the liberty of telling your cab driver that his services would be no longer needed. Come along. I promise to behave like a perfect gentleman.'

Sara shivered.

Instantly he was all concern. 'You are cold. I told you it was not wise to sit for long on the damp grass.'

She allowed him to take a light grip of her elbow and they walked to where he had parked his car. It was a long, opulent black one and he helped her into the front seat where she leaned back to the creak of expensive leather. She sat in her corner, gaining precious seconds like a prizefighter who had underestimated her opponent. She watched the strong brown fingers on the wheel of the car as it sprang forward into life like a well trained black panther. A delicate sensitive fear held her rigidly aware of her own defences being totally inadequate against a man who had everything in his favour.

Turning her head, Sara glimpsed blue skies, a sapphire sea and enough sunshine to melt the cold doubts around her heart as to her own resistance in her second round with the man beside her. Had anyone else been her companion she would have enjoyed the ride. But although his behaviour was impeccable, his remarks both witty and amusing, she was relieved when they returned to the hotel.

Helping her from the car, he took her hand to hold it firmly in his grasp.

'I have to go out this evening on business. What about a run to Nice tomorrow in the car?'

'I'm sorry,' she answered, and before he could say any more she withdrew her hand from his and ran up the steps into the hotel.

Patrice came to her room that evening as she was dressing.

'Have you had a nice day?' she asked, perching on the bed. 'It was quite nice in Grasse.' She gave a gurgle of amusement. 'I found Stewart about as exciting as Grandfather! No wonder you wanted to be rid of him. He's very fond of you, though.'

Sara slipped her dress over her head. 'Did he say so?'

'No, but I could tell. He quizzed me in a roundabout way, seemed to think I knew who you were going out with. He took it for granted you had a man in tow. Let me zip you up.'

Patrice stood up and zipped Sara into a mass of seagreen chiffon from which her shoulders rose with the velvety whiteness of magnolia petals. 'What a gorgeous dress! I can see Stewart's eyes boggling when he sees you.'

Sara smoothed the full skirt down over her slim hips, feeling no thrill of pleasure at the enchanting picture she made in the dressing table mirror. It was a delicately simple gown, classical in line with no ornamental and relying solely upon its exquisite cut. Her pale hair was combed up into a chignon, her make-up delicately applied, giving her skin a pearly glow.

She smiled suddenly at Patrice, enchanting in deep rose with her brown hair loose on her shoulders. 'Thanks, Patrice, but you look wonderful. That colour suits you. I'm pleased and very relieved to know you're not taken in by Stewart. He's a curious man, but he has his uses. Wouldn't you agree?'

She laughed, and Patrice laughed too.

'He's a good dancer,' she said.

'And that about sums him up,' murmured Sara.

Stewart was waiting for them at the entrance to the dining-room, and Sara ignored his look of appraisal. Knowing how he felt about her made her uneasy. She suppressed a shiver, forcing her attention back to the dining-room and the gentle flow of conversation amid the clinking of glasses. The room was filled this evening for the charity ball to be given later in the blue and gold ballroom.

They shared a table with two young Spaniards and Sara found herself seated by them. During the meal she laughed often at their absurd compliments which they tossed from her to Patrice, who was also in good form. Stewart was glum, but the time passed pleasantly enough for Sara.

After dinner they all trooped on to the terrace for coffee with the two young Spaniards tagging along. They spoke excellent English and were looking forward to the ball where they were to meet their fiancées, who were attending with a duenna.

In the ballroom decorated with tropical plants and flowers beneath crystal chandeliers Sara was at once surrounded by young men and whisked away as the music began. She had a glimpse of Stewart's set face as she drifted by, and saw Patrice dancing with a naval officer.

Sara did not see him again until just before the interval, when he made his way towards her as the dance number was ending. She had not wanted to dance with him. There was nothing to be gained by any kind of friendship between them, because it was not in her to be happy in his company.

'I suppose I may have a dance with you?' he said sarcastically.

'If you want to,' she answered lightly, allowing him to lead her away among the dancers as the next number began. 'Thanks for being nice to Patrice. She's sweet, and I would hate anything unpleasant to happen to her.'

'I agree. I could be nice to you if you'd let me.'

'Why should you?' Sarah had decided upon the light approach to keep him at bay. 'I would have thought you would want to steer clear of everything and everyone who reminded you of work. After all, you are on holiday.'

He made no reply and the dance ended – the last one before the interval. The idea of sitting it out with him and making polite conversation appalled her. Let him go to the bar, she thought, and excusing herself went up to the cloakroom to repair her make-up. She carried with her the memory of the unpleasant smile lifting the corners of his mouth, realizing that it was not so much actual dislike she felt for him at that moment as bitter resentment. He was spoiling her holiday. She found Patrice already in the cloakroom and they went downstairs together. In the bar they were at once caught up in a laughing, chattering crowd. A jolly-looking man asked them what they would like and an iced drink was pushed into their hands. Sara glimpsed Stewart at the far end of the room deep in conversation with two men who had the look of delegates about them and hoped she could steer clear of the man.

When they returned to the ballroom Sara and Patrice were claimed by partners who swung them away immediately. Sara's partner, an excellent dancer, told her he was in Monte Carlo to attend a conference the following day. As the evening wore on the dancers became riotously gay.

Paper flowers and streamers were flung around, and Sara was removing one from her head when she saw Armand across the room. The sudden sight of him jolted her. He did not look her way, being engrossed in something his companion was saying.

Michelle Despard's dark hair against the whiteness of his evening jacket was the last thing Sara saw as she moved round the room in the dance. It was getting late when her partner excused himself to go to make a telephone call and Sara slipped hastily into the grounds in order to avoid Stewart. Why should she dance with a man she did not like? Working at the same place with him did not give him the right to intrude into her private life.

She sighed. How lovely the grounds were, with the moon silvering the palm fronds and the illuminated windows of the ballroom shining out over the moonlit lawns. What a heavenly place it would be for a honeymoon! Dreamily, Sara pictured herself floating around the ballroom in the beloved's arms, then coming out for a short stroll before retiring. The sweet night air fragrant with the perfume of flowers gave her a nostalgic feeling for the company of someone belonging as the haunting sound of the last waltz jerked her back to reality.

It was a tune she was destined to remember. The last time Maura, Julian and herself had been together, they had danced to it on the occasion of the annual Hunt Ball. Sara shivered suddenly aware of the cold night air on her uncovered shoulders. She had been foolish to come outdoors without a wrap after the heat of the ballroom. And all because of Stewart Wilkes. She was either running from him or the horrid Frenchman. Her heart hardened when she thought of Armand.

Poor Maura had not stood a chance against him. The man was obviously a connoisseur of objets d'art, and that included women. He was probably on the look out for a pearl among women. Perhaps Michelle Despard. Sara quelled a second shiver and hastened her steps towards the front entrance of the hotel.

Suddenly she heard voices – a man's deep one and the slightly husky tones of a woman. The next moment a right-hand turn in the path between ornamental shrubs brought them face to face. Sara's eyes, dark blue and clear in the moonlight, stared up first at the woman then the man, unaware that the soft green fantasy of her evening gown gave her a look of ethereal loveliness. She stood there mutely, her hands by her sides, with Michelle's husky voice striking a discordant note on the clear night air.

'*Mon pavre enfant*, you must be frozen without a wrap. Are you running away from an unwelcome admirer?'

Hollow laughter, thought Sara, and almost congratulated Michelle on her accurate perception. She recovered herself with an effort, taking in Michelle's mink stole over her evening gown.

'I am on my way indoors and am quite comfortable, thanks,' she said quietly.

Her hands clenched as she met Armand's penetrating gaze with a look he rightly interpreted as defiant. Her lips tightened and her dislike of him sent the colour flooding her face. His white evening jacket threw into relief the deep tan of his face, giving it a chiselled look. The next moment his hand had shot out to grip her arm.

'*Mon dieu*,' he explained with a certain amount of irritation, 'you are frozen! What are you trying to do, catch a chill?'

'Armand, don't shout at the child!' Michelle gave a laugh which grated. But he was not listening. He was glowering down, conscious of the tremors running through Sara at his touch. Her aversion to him was so keen it was almost tangible. He was puzzled, she could tell.

'Is someone annoying you?' he demanded, looking formidable.

Sara gave a scathing look at the sudden tightening of his jaw and the thin line of his mouth. Then wriggling from his hold she disappeared like a wraith of sea mist through the grounds of the hotel.

Once in her room, she sat down on her bed and endeavoured to recover her breath. If she had behaved childishly she could only blame it on the tide of events since she had arrived in Monte Carlo. Bewildered and unhappy, Sara sat for a long time gazing into space and fighting a nostalgia for home and the placid companionship of her brother Julian. When he had told her of his intention to go abroad, Sara had thought that a holiday away from all her problems would help her to sort them out. Now she was not so sure, for it seemed that far from solving anything her problems had only increased since she had arrived in Monte Carlo.

Looking at the situation as it stood there were two courses open to her. She could either go on allowing the interference of two men whom she detested to ruin her holiday, or she could do something about it. Like someone pondering over a mathematical problem, Sara began with Armand. He was evidently out for what he could get, expert in handling women; he knew when to flatter and when to reject. Thinking about him dispassionately, Sara knew he had singled her out for his next affair. There could be no other reason, for he knew she was an ordinary working girl, not the kind, however beautiful, of whom his family would approve. Why not play him at his own game?

Granted she was not experienced in the art of love, but it was possible for her to ensnare him by her very innocence. She would be a novelty after his affairs with women as experienced as himself. Poor Maura had not been experienced, but that did not prove anything. Besides, by courting his interest she could rid herself of Stewart's unwelcome attentions. She might even get Armand to marry her. Then she could drop him and make him look a fool in the eyes of his friends. Why not? Revenge, a word which hitherto had held no meaning for Sara, sounded very sweet at that moment.

# CHAPTER THREE

Sara was up early for a swim in the outdoor pool the next morning with a view to outlining a plan of action. She breakfasted early, left a note under Patrice's door to say she was going out and left the hotel. At least the weather had been kind, for it was another beautiful sunny morning. With a sense of elation Sara walked to the forecourt of the palace to see the uniformed guards and strolled leisurely through magnificent gardens of tropical plants and flowers against a background of majestic mountains.

How much different life could be only by altering one's outlook, she thought, sitting down at a table at one of the pretty outdoor cafés in the narrow winding streets. After all, was it not Shakespeare who said something about the world being a stage on which we all played a part? All she had to do was to be totally unlike Armand's conception of a Parisienne; so utterly different from his experience of women. She ordered her coffee and sipped it thoughtfully.

And Armand, glancing towards the café on his way to the harbour, saw her slight figure, her fair hair gleaming in the sun, with practically no artifice. She had what he could only describe as a look of pathos, a solitary look which should not have been there in the face of one so young.

Although he greeted her quietly, he knew he had startled her. It was evident by the flush of embarrassment on her face as she lifted a wide-eyed glance.

'Good morning, Miss Everette. Enjoying the sunshine? I trust your foot is better?'

He touched the peak of his uniform hat in a mocking salute. Beneath the back shiny peak his black eyes danced devilishly as a golden finger of sun touched his handsome face and brilliant smile. He was wearing the uniform of a yachtsman, making him more definite, tangible and disturbing. He had an exciting effect upon her which no man had ever had before, but stoically, Sara put this down to what she knew about him. The thing was to play it cool.

She returned his audacious greeting with a cool smile. 'My foot is better, thanks. Don't let me detain you.'

'You are not. Mind if I join you?'

'Do,' she answered sweetly. 'I was just leaving.'

He sat down, lifting a sardonic brow at her barely touched coffee. 'You are not leaving your coffee, surely? Drink it up and have one with me.'

Sara, about to rise to her feet, hesitated, and was restrained by some inner force stronger than herself bidding her to stay. If she had any qualms at the game she was about to play they were swept away by his look of arrogant charm. Certainly this attractive Frenchman needed teaching a lesson.

'No more coffee for me, thanks,' she said hurriedly as the waiter approached for his order. 'One is sufficient.'

He bowed sardonically to her command and ordered one for himself. Watching her curiously, he wondered what it was that, a moment before, had caused her hesitation and caused her to stay.

'We seem fated to meet,' he drawled when the waiter had brought his coffee with incredible speed. 'Actually, I am on my way to the harbour to try out a boat for a friend of mine who is hoping to use it when he comes. Do you like sailing, Miss Everette?'

'I like the sea,' she said evasively.

'Then what about going with me? The sea is as smooth as a millpond this morning. You will enjoy it.'

Sara drank the rest of her coffee and put down her cup decisively. 'No, thanks.'

'Why not? You are here on holiday, so why not make the most of it? I have seen you bathing in the pool at the hotel and you strike me as being the typical outdoor kind. Why sit about like some staid old lady when there is so much to do and so little time to do it?' He leaned forward tantalizingly. 'The only strenuous thing I have seen you do so far is avoiding me.'

'Surely what I chose to do on my holiday is my own affair?' she said stiltedly.

He raised a dark ironic brow. 'Do you not want to hire a horse, play squash, golf or tennis, go skating on an indoor rink, go fishing or explore the countryside?' he asked with a wry humour.

The colour flooded her face and neck. Here she was, practically planning to seduce the man into marriage and doing nothing about it. His smile encompassed her with its warmth and tenderness as his personality surrounded her like a net affecting her both physically and mentally, attaining substance. Her thoughts were chaotic. Here he was offering her the opportunity she wanted. He was obviously at a loose end. Now was her chance.

'You are coming for a sail with me,' he said firmly. 'If only to throw those troubles of yours overboard.'

He drank his coffee and rose to his feet. Sara followed suit, capitulating to the inevitable. Nervously, she was aware of him slowing down his long stride to accommodate her smaller steps and they left the crowded thoroughfare to make for the harbour.

In the harbour, among other equally immaculate vessels, was the *Neptune*. Armand dropped on deck and reached up to swing her on board beside him. In no time with the minimum of effort he had the gleaming ketch, her sails straining, gliding effortlessly seawards. All around them seagulls screeched, swooped and dived like huge scraps of paper as they sailed over the sparkling water with Sara's face just below the level of his shoulder.

Sara was normally a gay person with an imp of mischief dancing in her blue eyes. But since Maura's tragic death her sparkle had only emerged on occasions in a truant smile. Now, standing on the sloping deck of the magnificent ketch and watching three snowy white sails fill with wind and tasting the salt spray on her lips, Sara felt on top of the world. The invigorating breeze brought a soft bloom to her face as she lifted it to meet the refreshing spray and closed her eyes. She opened them again to find Armand looking down at her intently. And those few moments lost in his dark eyes almost lulled her into forgetting the misery and unhappiness he had caused. With a deep intensity of feeling which was almost a pain, Sara knew that had she met him today for the first time with no bitter memories between them, it was quite possible for her to have fallen in love with him.

'Enjoying it?' he asked above the wind, amused by her glowing cheeks and shining eyes.

Sara laughed, half sad, half gay, with enchanting dimples appearing in the soft curves of her cheeks. 'Very much,' she answered. The air went to her head like a first taste of champagne. She was young enough to live entirely for the moment even though that moment was tinged with bitter memories.

Neither of them spoke much. It was enough to take in the air and fill their lungs like vitamins. When they returned to the harbour, Armand sprang on to the quay and hauled her up beside him. His car was parked nearby and in no time at all they were back at the hotel. They parted in the foyer.

'*A bientôt*, Miss Everette,' he said, and went striding to the reception desk obviously to make some inquiry, leaving Sara to make her way upstairs to change for lunch.

She was rather surprised and a little piqued that he had not made arrangements to see her again. Quite obviously this past master of affairs with women worked to a routine. Probably he would not approach her again for a day or so until she began to miss his charming attentions.

Patrice joined her for dinner in the dining-room that evening. Stewart had taken her to Nice for the day but was not coming down to dinner. He was not feeling too well.

Patrice said, 'He was awfully disappointed when I told him you'd gone out this morning. He seems to have caught a chill and said he wouldn't come down to dinner. I wanted to go up to the Alps to see the skiing championships, but Stewart isn't interested in winter sports. You know there's a helicopter service operating from the beach here that gets you there in no time.'

39

Sara was interested. 'Really? Do you ski, Patrice?'

Patrice smiled. 'Yes, and it's great fun. Do you?'

Sara shook her head. 'No, but it sounds good fun to try.'

'It is, and easy to learn if you're keen enough. After a week of expert tuition you can really begin to enjoy yourself.'

'You sound experienced.'

Patrice tried to look modest and failed. Her laughter tinkled. 'Seeing that I've lived in Switzerland all my life . . .' she began.

'How silly of me not to have guessed,' Sara broke in. 'I'd love to go with you. What shall I need in the way of clothes? I've brought an anorak, a heavy white cable sweater and some ski pants, remembering that sometimes it snows even in April.' She laughed lightly. 'I came prepared.'

'That's fine.' Patrice was delighted. 'You can hire the rest when you get there. Don't forget your sunglasses.'

'I won't. Did you say there was some kind of tournament?'

'Yes, the last before the snow goes. We could go skiing in the morning and watch the championships in the afternoon. We can order an early breakfast in our room in order to make an early start.'

Sara enjoyed that evening. She went to the cabaret with Patrice and danced later to the hotel band. Later, going to her room, Sara went on to her balcony drawn there by the beauty of the night. The evening sky was bright with stars, the moon, king size, lending a sense of unreality to a small state which might have come out of a fairy tale. She leaned back against the frame of the French window and hoped Julian was not feeling too lonely, wherever he was at that moment. She wished fervently that soon he might meet some woman who would help him forget Maura. Maybe she would go out there herself next year to see him. She might even stay. Suddenly, cigarette smoke mingling with the perfumed air drew her eyes downwards to a lower balcony two floors beneath her own. The unexpected sight of the wide shoulders and the arrogant angle of the well-shaped dark head jolted her into life.

Armand, smoking a cigarette and gazing pensively at the view, appeared to be deep in thought. Instinctively, Sara drew back, wondering what he was thinking. Certainly not of poor Maura. A tight little cord knotted in her throat. She saw his shoulders pull back in a firm movement of muscles as he flung away the butt of his cigarette as if reaching a decision. Well, she had too! Sara set her teeth hard and all her body became rigid. Her plan for revenge still stood. It was the only way to settle her mind about Maura – the only way to stop the tragedy of her friend's death from tormenting her. As she turned blindly into her room Sara found herself hating Armand Romond de Poulain as she had never hated anyone in her life.

After breakfast the next morning, Sara, clad in ski pants, sweater and anorak, opened the door to Patrice clad in same offering her a gay little woollen hat in red with a pom-pom like the one she herself was wearing.

'Thanks, Patrice. How sweet of you.' Sara pulled the cap on over her fair hair. Then picking up her bag containing all she would need for the day, she said, 'We'd better ring Stewart up to ask how he is. You do it, Patrice. That way he won't have wrong ideas.'

'I see what you mean.'

Patrice picked up the phone, had a few words with Stewart and told him they were going to the Alps for the day. 'He's staying in bed today to rid himself of his cold,' she said as she put down the phone.

The trip to the Alps in the helicopter was a journey into fairyland for Sara. They whirred from shade into brilliant sunshine over snow-smothered trees, skyscraper cliffs and white deserts of snow right into a basin of blue sky innocent of cloud. The helicopter put them down near the tiny town and they made for the ski equipment shop.

There they were able to hire sturdy leather boots battened down by huge metal clips, thick woollen stockings and warm leather gloves. Then with a crowd of enthusiastic skiers they caught the cable car to the gentle slopes for beginners not far from the steep inclines occupied by the experts.

Sara waved to Patrice who, with the experienced skiers, made for the summit among a sea of brown faces topped by gaily coloured caps, and found herself among the paler faces of the beginners. The instructor was a handsome young man named Anton who soon put her at her ease. Slim, agile and eager to learn, Sara listened carefully to his instructions.

First it was a matter of balance and going up the slope sideways with skis on. Exercises like going down lifting one foot at a time and hopping about like a kangaroo followed. Eventually one learned the 'snow-plough'. This meant coming downhill with the toes of the skis together and the heels splayed wide apart in order to regulate the speed. Reaching the end of the run was rather confusing, like turning left when you turned right in a flurry of snow.

Spills were inevitable, but Sara loved it. The time went on wings and she was surprised when Patrice came all aglow and ready for lunch. After lunch, they spent another hour on the slopes in the pure thin air before shedding their skis and going for the traditional drink.

On the terrace of a restaurant high up in the summit they sipped hot wine with lemon and watched the highlight of the day, a tournament with top skiers taking part. Level with the high plateau from which the skiers took their terrifying leaps into the vast space below, they watched and applauded. A loudspeaker called out the names of each competitor and the scores went up on a board.

One by one the skiers cut through the air with superb skill and judgment to loud applause. Sara had been vastly interested in a blond young giant whom Patrice had been regarding with more than casual impartiality when the next competitor put them both out of her mind. It was Armand, and from the storm of applause greeting him, he was obviously very popular. With a brilliant smile on his tanned face, he stood at the top of the dangerous run adjusting his goggles. His leap through the air and his landing were perfect and merited the highest marks on the scoreboard for a performance without precedence.

Sara was not surprised. He gave the impression of attaining any goal he set out for with the minimum of effort. There was a kind of ruthlessness about him which made for perfection. Again she found it hard to reconcile a man of his forceful character with the no-good whom Maura had loved.

She did not see him again before they left the slopes to return to the hotel for dinner that evening. She dined with Patrice, after which they went to the ballroom. The day spent in the high altitude of the Alps, far from tiring Sara, seemed to have rejuvenated her. She flitted from one partner to another feeling on a cloud when, between dances, she saw Armand making his way across the room towards her. Vital and glowing, he brought with him the freshness of mountain air along with his brilliant smile. His ruddy bronze skin was enhanced by his recent sojourn in the Alps and his greeting was skilfully casual.

Low and vibrantly, he requested the pleasure of a dance, and she was in his arms before she could gather her confused thoughts. He danced superbly with the ease of active muscles, his hold correct, his manner courteous. A woman did not stand an earthly chance of resisting him, Sara thought despairingly, vaguely aware of Patrice dancing with the young blond giant she had been so interested in at the tournament.

Never in her wildest dreams had Sara found dancing so exquisite a pleasure. So attuned was she, so responsive to his every move, that every fibre of her being was aware of him. Vainly she tried to convince herself that the strange emotion she was experiencing lay purely in the pleasure of the dance. It was the result of overtiredness, a kind of delirium brought on by an exciting day, and nothing to do with her partner.

He claimed the last three dances and steered her masterfully in the direction of the hotel bar at the end.

'A nightcap before going to bed,' he said.

Sara, still dazed, found herself among a happy chattering crowd filling the bar. Then Armand was introducing her to a couple who occupied high stools at the far end of the bar.

'Miss Sara Everette, Maurice and Michelle Despard,' he said suavely, and ordered drinks for four as Maurice Despard gave Sara his seat.

She acknowledged their greeting politely, recognizing Armand's former companion in the hotel. How far had his affair with the chic Frenchwoman gone? she thought wryly. She liked Maurice Despard and imagined most women did. Of medium height and squarely built, he had a twinkle in his eye, an air of amusement about him as if he found everything around him vastly entertaining. His brown hair receded a little from his forehead to form a centre point, his face was square, frankly revealing and wholly charming.

'I saw you on the nursery slopes today, Miss Everette. You did very well,' he said with a twinkle.

Sara blushed. 'My first lessons taken mostly sitting down,' she said demurely. 'Thanks,' this as Armand handed her a drink, dark eyebrows raised.

'You were skiing today, Miss Everette?' he said.

She chuckled. 'Kind of. I'm awfully relieved to know you didn't see me.'

Armand dispensed the rest of the drinks and took one for himself before answering. 'Why not? Everyone has to learn.'

Sara smiled. 'Judging by your performance today I would say you were born to it. What do you say, Monsieur Despard? Do you ski?'

He grimaced nicely. 'So-so. My wife is the enthusiast. I am lazy and much prefer to sip wine and watch other people live dangerously.'

Sara mischievously raised her glass. 'To you then, Monsieur Despard, and many pleasant hours of watching the fun.' Her look at Armand was coolly polite. 'To you, Monsieur Romond de Poulain, for your excellent performance today – Madame Despard.'

Michelle's smile was as warm as Sara's. They drank the toast, then Armand was murmuring in her ear, 'Why did I not see you on the slopes? Were you hiding behind some snow-smothered bush?'

'The nursery slopes are way out of your domain, monsieur. I doubt if you ever knew them.'

The expression in his dark eyes sent the colour rushing to her face – as he had meant it to do, she thought furiously.

Coolly, he turned to Michelle. 'Did you see Miss Everette on the slopes today, Michelle?'

Michelle allowed a sip of wine to sip down her long elegant throat before replying. 'I returned from an enjoyable run to find my husband watching Miss Everette through his binoculars. He was evidently enchanted,' she answered dryly, looking at her grinning husband. 'His interest set me wondering whether he does that kind of thing regularly.'

'Do you, Maurice?' Armand was grinning also at his friend. 'It seems there is more to supping wine than meets the eye. Remind me to try it some time.'

Maurice was in no way perturbed. 'You are far too good on the entertainment side. Your performance today was brilliant. You had the women swooning at your feet.'

Armand flicked a mocking glance at Sara. 'Miss Everette would not agree with you. She dislikes me intensely and rebuffs all my efforts to be friendly.'

The wine and her determination to better this audacious Frenchman gave Sara the courage to ignore him. Her eyes neither sought nor avoided his, but gave an impression of complete indifference.

'Then beware, Miss Everette.' It was Maurice speaking. 'You are living dangerously when you challenge Armand. Incidentally, I often watch the beginners on the nursery slopes. Their antics are hilariously funny at times. Yours I found perfectly delightful. There you were in your gay little bobbed cap, all fierce determination to conquer or die. Your movements were a mixture of glowing enthusiasm and sparkle. Indeed, I enjoyed your performance as much as I enjoyed Armand's. Are you staying at the hotel, Miss Everette?'

45

'Yes. I have seen your wife on occasions, but not you.'

'He was probably watching you from behind some potted palm in his binoculars,' Armand put in audaciously.

Maurice ignored this with a wicked grimace. 'I arrived yesterday. I sent Michelle along earlier to warm the bed. We busy people have to take our holidays when we can, and I much prefer mine at high summer.'

They all laughed at this and Michelle said frankly, 'My husband is a consultant surgeon, Miss Everette, and it is quite a feat to lever him away from his work. I hope you are staying long enough to feel the benefit, Maurice. You need the break.'

Sara noted the lines of strain around his eyes and mouth and put his age at around forty. Michelle was a well preserved thirty or so, and likeable. She had looked tenderly upon her husband and Sara sensed a strong bond of affection between them which made her feel strangely lonely. Michelle's whole manner gave her a sense of ease, mitigating the fact that they were strangers. Her gown was as expensive as those around her and her jewels were certainly not paste.

Both men had all the *tournure* of well-bred Frenchmen, but it was Armand's deep voice with its foreign intonation which affected her most. They discussed the tournament and the merits of skiing while Sara listened, waiting for an opportunity to leave them. It came when Maurice suggested another drink.

'Not for me, thanks,' she told him hastily. 'I'm quite happy to call it a day.'

Armand bent his head. 'Am I forgiven?' he asked in a low voice meant for her ears alone.

Sara met his intent gaze coolly. 'For what?'

'For treading on your foot and for invading your solitude. I shall be on my best behaviour when we go out tomorrow.'

Sara's smile became a little fixed. 'I wasn't aware that we were going out tomorrow.'

'It's a pleasure in store for you, and one you can dream

46

about tonight.'

'And what is it Miss Everette can dream about?' Michelle asked after a short conversation with her husband.

'Ask Monsieur Romond de Poulain,' Sara said. 'I'm off to bed. Good night.'

She had entered her room when Patrice came behind her, sparkling and in the mood to gossip.

'I've been waiting for you to come up.' She closed the door behind her. 'You didn't say you knew Armand when we were at the tournament this afternoon, Sara.'

'I don't know him very well. Anyway, it's not important, is it?' She moved across the room to the dressing-table and Patrice followed.

'Not really.' Patrice peered into the mirror anxiously. 'Oh dear, not another pimple just when I want to look my best!' she exclaimed tragically.

Sara took off her ear-rings and put them down on the dressing-table. 'Who for? Not the dashing Stewart, surely. Or is it the dishy Armand?'

'Good heavens, no! Armand is a pet, but he's at least thirty.'

Sara chuckled. 'Almost senile!'

'Remember the young blond man who went before Armand in the tournament?'

Sara nodded and smiled impishly. 'The one you were swooning over?'

Patrice stared in horror. 'Goodness, was I so transparent?'

'I was only kidding. Do stop squeezing that pimple. You'll only enlarge the pores.' She drew down Patrice's hands from her face. 'Weren't you dancing with him tonight?'

'Yes. I've known him for years. He taught me how to ski and we were firm friends until he went away to college. Then we lost touch.'

'Do go on,' Sara urged her encouragingly.

Patrice toyed with the ear-rings. 'He's asked me to go skiing with him tomorrow.'

'That's wonderful. How much do you like him? Enough to go?'

'More than that, much more. Johan is four years older than me. I think I have loved him all my life.' Patrice hesitated, then the words came out with a rush. 'I wasn't entirely honest with you about my reason for staying on at the hotel. I had an idea that Johan would be taking part in the tournament yesterday, and that is the real reason I stayed on at the hotel.'

'Then you're going with him skiing tomorrow?'

'But what about you?'

'I don't enter into it – if you mean going skiing. While I would love to go I'm afraid my money would not run to another flip in the helicopter and a day in the Alps, thanks all the same,' Sara said dryly. 'I hope you have a good time. I'm also very happy that things have turned out as you wanted them to. You didn't have to tell me anything. Only enough to give me the idea I was doing the right thing in encouraging you to stay after your grandfather had gone. But do take care tomorrow. I'd like to think of you going home in one piece.'

Patrice beamed. 'I shall – and thanks, Sara. You're very sweet.'

Sara looked suddenly thoughtful. 'What about travelling back home with your blond skier? That way you wouldn't have to explain to your parents why you didn't go home after your grandfather left. You could say you stopped for the championships.'

'What a good idea!' Patrice kissed Sara's cheek. 'See you tomorrow night.' She paused at the door. 'About Stewart? I feel a little guilty about deserting him. I shall buy him a present before I leave.'

'Do,' Sara agreed. 'Get your young man to help you select something suitable. Might make him jealous!'

# CHAPTER FOUR

SARA awoke the next morning feeling stiff in every joint after the skiing lessons of the previous day, and decided to go for a bathe in the swimming pool. Putting on her swim suit and covering it with her towelling jacket, she went downstairs. The pool was warm and there were not above half a dozen heads bobbing in the water when she slipped off her robe. Gradually, the stiffness of her limbs became less acute and the gentle lap of the water filled her with a sense of wellbeing.

She swam for a while leisurely before pulling herself out on to the side of the pool. She was in a brown study wondering how to spend her day when a familiar voice said, 'Come on in, Miss Everette. Do not sit there looking at it.'

Armand was below her treading water and pushing back his hair from his face. Sara was irritated beyond measure to find her heart suddenly beating a tattoo against her ribs. Why should she be affected by the black challenging eyes of a man she had every reason to despise? As she met his half insolent, half probing gaze, she felt the rising tide of colour flooding her face. So he had decided to seek her out again. Of course he would be at a loose end since his girl-friend's husband had arrived.

'I've already been in the water and I was thinking of going to breakfast,' she informed him coldly. Then she slipped into the water and swam deliberately to the spot where she had left her towelling jacket. Hauling herself up out of the water, she hastened to put it on. Apparently intent upon tying the belt around her small waist, she was aware against her will of him landing beside her, aware of the rippling muscles beneath his gleaming skin of polished bronze with not an ounce of superfluous flesh.

'I shall begin to think you are scared of me,' he murmured, looking amused.

There was something young and appealing about her

dignity as she answered without looking at him. 'You would be wise not to think anything where I am concerned. You might get more than you bargained for.'

This seemed to amuse him still more. He shrugged into his robe not far away from where hers had been and looked down at her mockingly as he tied the belt. 'You would be surprised the times I have hoped that I might be getting just that, but I have always been disappointed.'

'Hard luck. I suggest you keep on trying, but not with me.'

When she would have turned to leave him his hand shot out and closed with a deceptive lazy hold on her wrist.

'Are you going skiing today?'

'No, I'm not.'

Sara wriggled against his grip and encountered the enigmatic expression in his dark eyes. Anger? Fear? Dislike? She was in no fit state to analyse the emotions which sent her heart lurching against her chest.

'And you're not going with me today.' The black brows lifted. 'Pity – we might have had fun.'

Seconds went by while he took his time looking down into her flushed face. Then slowly he released her wrist. Thus freed, Sara lost no time in putting space between them. Was she afraid of him? Engrossed in her thoughts, she was stepping into the lift before she realized someone had been calling her name. It was the receptionist coming on morning duty, and he hurried after her with a letter.

'I am sorry, Miss Everette,' he said politely. 'This letter came for you yesterday and was put in the wrong slot by mistake. I trust it will cause no inconvenience to you.'

Sara took the letter, recognized her brother's writing and saw the London postmark. She smiled. 'No. It's perfectly all right, thanks very much.'

Wondering why Julian should send her a letter before he left for California, Sara read it as soon as she reached her room.

Dear Sara, I send this letter with the hope that you will thoroughly enjoy your holiday. I know you'll miss me far more than if Maura had been with you. However, I'm inclined to think that you'll be all the better for being on your own, for you spent far too much time with me, time which you might have spent with some nice chap who will eventually give you a home and family. The little gift I enclose goes with all my love. Buy something with it that gives you the most pleasure. Be happy, Sara. As for me, I'm doing something I always wanted to do, work abroad for experience. This new post offers unlimited prospects and I'm really thrilled about it. So get cracking and send me that letter saying you've met the man in your life, who may be nearer than you think at this very moment. God bless, Julian.

Inside the letter was a cheque for a hundred pounds. Sara saw it through a blur of tears. How sweet of him! She sat looking at it for some time until she realized she could now afford to go skiing after all. And why not? She would enjoy it. It was not yet half past seven, still time for an early breakfast in her room before she went down to the helicopter leaving at eight-thirty.

There was no sign of Patrice or Johan on the helicopter. They were not likely to meet in any case, since the nursery slopes were not in the path of the more experienced skiers. Today, as yesterday, the mountains shone in a sea of white crisp snow overlaid by the yellow cast of the sun.

'Not long now before the snows melt,' remarked the pilot on landing them near the tiny town. 'Have fun!'

The man at the ski equipment store remembered Sara from the previous day and soon fixed her up. Then happily, with her breath sending out frosty signals of steam in the thin air, she clumped her way to the cable car waiting to take her to the slopes. Julian's letter and his gift had lifted her spirits higher than they had been for a long time and she was really enjoying herself.

Anton greeted her when she arrived with a flashing smile, pleased, he said, to see she had returned for more punishment. He teased her in excellent English and put her through her paces with the rest of the beginners. Then came the moment of pure joy when she was able to turn round at the top of the slope with all the poise and balance of a professional, run her skis backwards and forwards to ensure they were sliding well and proceed to go gently down the slope.

The swish of the skis, the creak of snow-laden branches of smothered trees, and the cries of learners when they came a cropper at the end of the run were the only sounds in Sara's ears for the next few hours. Breathlessly, she would pause on reaching the top of the slopes, and look up at the soaring peaks to see star skiers, their stomachs levelled to the ground, plunging down almost perpendicular inclines. Then she would turn from the sublime to the ridiculous to look down on the learners spinning round on stomachs and backs like hapless jellyfish as they came a cropper at the end of the run.

Leaning forward on her skis, Sara was about to push off down the incline for the umpteenth time when a figure levelled to the ground, plunging down almost perfect finish at the foot of the run with scarcely a flurry of snow.

'Come on, Miss Everette, show me what you can do!'

The deep tones echoing through the clear thin air hit her ears like a pistol shot. The gay sounds around her faded into the background until there were just two people up there among the soaring peaks, Armand and herself.

Her lips compressed as she stared down at his laughing devil-may-care face. If only she had his skill! 'How you would love to see me fall!' she called. 'Well, look out you probably will. After all, we aren't all experts.'

Determinedly, Sara kept her balance and pushed herself forward. The downward plunge brought a heady delight, but as she neared the bottom of the slopes she could not quite recall when the breaking should start to bring about a perfect finish, Armand's mocking gaze did not help. The result was an undignified sprawl in the snow.

He lifted her with a deep chuckle, adjusted her gay little bobbled hat which had fallen down over her eyes and dusted her free of snow as he would a child.

'So you've fallen for me at last,' he quipped. 'Not hurt, are you?'

Sara shook her head, furious at her own submissiveness. She hardly recognized herself as the woman who had been aflame to have her revenge on him, to hurt him as he had hurt Maura. But one glance of the black eyes, the masterful mouth and lean tanned face had reduced her to a kind of mindless puppet.

With a blob of snow on her sweet little nose, she blinked her eyelashes free of it and stared at him, her blue eyes sparkling and clear in her rosy, animated face.

'You look about ten,' he said as though it annoyed him. 'Sure you're not hurt?'

A dimple appeared. 'No, I'm not hurt. After all, I am on the nursery slopes.' She braved the glitter in the dark eyes. 'Bit of a comedown for you, though.'

He grinned. 'It was for you a moment ago. I'm glad you did not break a limb, although it would have anchored you down. Think you can make it to the cable car on your skis?'

Sara looked down at unknown territory, a white blanket of innocent white snow always formidable to a beginner, then lifted her small chin defiantly.

'Like to bet?' This was the real Sara speaking, someone she had not revealed in her previous encounters with him. Her sudden lightheartedness was making subterfuge impossible.

He raised a mocking brow. 'A kiss that you do not make it, *ma petite*, without a spill.' His look was openly challenging, the dark eyes twinkled wickedly. 'It is a fairly easy run down, with a few trees on the way. If you do end up by embracing one, I will not hold it against you. You have only to follow me and do as I do.'

'How magnanimous of you,' she said demurely. 'Lead on, monsieur.'

He went down with the relaxed precision of the expert, leaving a perfect example of feather-stitching in the snow punctuated perfectly by the pricks of his poles. An awfully long way down, or so it seemed to Sara, he swept round into a perfect turn to halt and stood looking up

53

waiting for her to join him.

His very perfection was enough to daunt even her kind of courage. But Sara was no coward. She would go down fighting if fall she must. Barely an outward quiver ruffled her air of bravado, although there were butterflies in her stomach. With her knees bent, her shins pressing forward on the top of her boots and her slim form balanced somewhere around her midriff, Sara pushed her way downwards, regulating her speed to one she could control. Following his tracks painstakingly, she reached the bottom of the slope, swept round in a perfect parallel and halted, still on her feet.

Armand grinned. 'Well done!' he cried.

It was difficult to say who was the most surprised. Sara was speechless. His sudden embrace was enchanting, his face cold from the invigorating air, his mouth lingering no more than seconds. Immediately her head jerked back. The blue eyes flashed fire.

'That's cheating,' she cried scornfully. 'I won the bet.'

He grinned. 'The kiss, if you can call it one, was a salute to your performance, *ma petite*. It was excellent.'

He took off his skis, helped Sara with hers and putting them on his shoulder, flicked her a curious glance. 'I thought you were not coming to the slopes today?'

'I changed my mind.'

'I am pleased you did. And now for lunch. I do not know about you, but I am famished!'

Sara found she was too. The exhilarating air and the exercise had filled her with a sense of wellbeing which gave her no time for unhappy thought. They met Patrice and Johan in the restaurant. Armand and Johan knew each other and all four shared a table. During the meal Patrice gave Sara a wink. She, no doubt, thought Armand had brought her to the slopes, and the meal passed pleasantly.

Later, Patrice and Johan went skiing and Armand stayed to coach Sara. He was a wonderful teacher and she enjoyed herself. She was often breathless, and not wholly

54

on account of the vigorous exercise, for she forgot her antagonism against him and lived only for the moment. But later, over cream cakes and mulled wine as they waited for the helicopter to take them back, memories again sprang painfully back to life, tormenting Sara with their vividness. Armand's presence was a constant reminder of all she had lost through him in the way of companionship, and she felt lonelier than ever in the laughter and chatter around her.

Back at the hotel, she thanked him for an enjoyable day.

'The day is not yet over,' he reminded her, holding on to her hand firmly. 'I shall be dining with you this evening. And will you call me Armand?'

The sound of his name on her lips affected her oddly and with a feeling of having burned her boats, she capitulated. 'Very well, Armand.'

As she entered her room, Sara wondered why she felt a swift feeling of inflation after a strangely exciting day filled with colour and promise. A deep sense of loss of a different kind than she had experienced since Maura and Julian had gone sent a hollow ache inside her. Apart from her father and brother, she had never loved any other man. The entry of Armand into her life had alerted her to wonderful things which might have happened had he been anyone but Armand Romond de Poulain.

Thoughtfully, Sara walked across her room to the balcony and gazed out sadly. She would be playing a dangerous game in encouraging him. The thought held her rigid as if she had come unawares upon a danger which not only menaced Armand but herself. She knew that while her association with him could bring joy ecstacy, it could also bring sorrow and desolation if she allowed her interest in him to grow.

Her hands trembled as she dressed for dinner that evening, preparing herself for what she knew would be an ordeal, a test of her own powers of dissimulation. The deep amber of her dress brought out the colour of the pale gold hair folded demurely in a French pleat at the back of her small head. Her make-up had been sparingly applied and the whole effect was perfectly charming.

She entered the lift with an apparent casualness and met Armand with perfect composure in the foyer. Walking towards him with her quick light step, she was a picture of cool, fresh, enchanting young womanhood. When Louis escorted them to the table behind the palms she had chosen on her first night in the hotel, Armand smiled at her mockingly. All through the meal he was conscious of his intent gaze, his deep enchanting voice.

He proved an amusing companion, relating amusing incidents on the skiing runs which caused her to shake with quiet laughter. 'Cigarette?' he asked, offering his case when they had reached the coffee stage.

Sara refused. Idiotically, she was reminded of smoking the pipe of peace, something she could never do with a man who had cost her friend her life.

'I find it refreshing to come across someone like you with the strength of character to be moderate in things.' He leaned back in his chair, exhaled smoke and regarded her between narrowed lids. 'All the same, I wish you would relax. You hold yourself much too aloof, clam up if the conversation touches your personal life and act like a closed book. Usually, I enjoy a good book, but yours appears to be reserved for some more fortunate fellow.'

Sara managed a smile. 'I'm sure you would find my book a very ordinary one, quite out of place with the colourful ones you must have collected over the years.'

'My women friends usually leave their troubles behind when they dine with me. As for my experience with them, I am thirty-one years of age and there would be something seriously wrong with me had I reached that age without dabbling in a few affairs.'

'And you're still not married?'

'No. Should I be?'

Sara shrugged and drank the rest of her coffee. 'One wonders why you have never succumbed to some charmer.'

He smiled wisely. 'Women can attract men up to a certain point and yet not succeed in getting the men to take them seriously enough for marriage. A man looks for something special in a woman and does not find it. Maybe he will go on looking all his life and not find it. I shall probably find what I seek in a Frenchwoman as you will in an Englishman – shall we say like the one who was with you at the swimming pool the other day.'

So he had been more observant than he had seemed to be after that first impersonal glance across the pool. However, the idea of marrying someone even remotely like Stewart made her recoil so much with horror that the words were out before she could control them.

'Heaven forbid! I can't stand the man.'

He raised dark level brows. 'No? He did appear to be rather a dull stick.' Suddenly he leaned forward, his dark eyes glittering oddly. 'So you do not want a dull stick and I appear to frighten you off. Would you say someone between the two of us might suit, or have you already decided upon your future husband?'

Sara froze, said coldly, 'Why should I tell you about my personal affairs?'

He tapped a finger of ash from his cigarette into the ash tray provided, lazily.

'Because I am most intrigued.'

'Then I won't disillusion you.'

'And you will not tell me?'

Sara drank the rest of her coffee, instinctively on her guard against him. He was too perceptive, too critical, looking down at her with his penetrating gaze. His arrogant remark that he would choose a Frenchwoman for his wife, to her way of thinking, brushed off the Englishwoman as negligible, even inferior. It roused her fighting spirit until she felt she wanted to show him that Englishwomen did not fall short in any way against their French counterparts. They could be just as feminine and desirable.

He leaned forward, crushing out the butt of his cigarette in the ash tray.

'I suggest as it is a perfect evening for a run in the car that we take full advantage of it. After a rather strenuous day perhaps you would prefer it to dancing? Or would you prefer to go to a show?' He smiled. 'I promise not to tread on your feet if you want to dance.'

Sara lifted her head and regarded him steadily. The well-shaped head on the wide shoulders – the dark eyes, piercing and intelligent, the firm jawline and the well defined mouth, told her he was a man who would be baulked at nothing. The thought started the sickening little current of antagonism which had run through her bloodstream against him when she had read Maura's last letter.

Sara took a steadying breath. Maybe she was being foolish in allowing her friend's death to fill her with a fierce urge of revenge. Just how foolish she dare not contemplate. But she had to do something to relieve the bitterness. She thought despairingly, If only I knew for certain that he had treated Maura badly. If he had not, then what she was going to do would be very wrong. On the other hand, if he had . . .

Her chin rose and her smile was utterly sweet. 'The car run, please . . . Armand.'

He did not answer Not immediately. Instead, he looked at her quizzically, almost as if he was aware that the truce between them was temporary.

'As you wish,' he said at last with a studied courtesy. But his eyes said, 'You can smile at me provocatively now, but later, when we are alone, do not blame me!'

A cold shiver of apprehension feathered across her skin when his cool fingers touched her neck as he dropped the evening wrap about her shoulders. Outside the hotel entrance they saw a young couple mounting the steps. So absorbed were they in each other that they failed to notice Sara and Armand as they passed. It was Patrice and Johan. Armand lifted an ironic brow, but Sara envied their absorption in each other.

Armand's car was in the hotel parking ground. He helped her in, slammed her door and walked round the front to take his place beside her. The car purred forward, circled and slid away down the driveway to the main road where it gathered speed. Sara leaned back luxuriously in the spacious seat to the creak of expensive leather. The gay lights receded and they swept along a well-made road between tall palms rustling gently in the faint breeze.

Armand had abandoned his former teasing mood and drove in silence. Sara sat beside him, her hands clasped loosely in her lap, watching the road ahead curve, straighten and curve again like a live thing.

He spoke at length in formal pleasant tones. 'Have you your passport with you, Sara?' He flicked an amused look at her surprised face. 'I ask because we could visit the casino, if you have.'

Sara had known it was imperative when in a foreign country to carry your passport with you.

'Have you a car?' he asked presently.

'No. But I can drive. It isn't much fun driving in London – too much traffic.'

He threw her another swift glance. 'So you live in London. With your parents?'

'I have no parents. I have a flat. I'm a secretary and I live alone.'

'Like it?'

Sara twisted her hands together nervously as she thought back to the time when she had loved her job because Maura and Julian were there.

'It's interesting,' she replied laconically.

Another of those brief glances. 'Ever thought of marrying?'

'Not particularly.'

He drove in silence at an excessive speed which Sara did not find in the least frightening. His superb control of the big car made the speed seem perfectly normal. She wondered what destination he had in mind, then saw they were pulling in at a kind of beer-cellar where one could drink wine and dance in dimly lit rooms to mountain music. Judging by the opulent cars parked nearby it was a very popular stopping place. Later they went to the little casino at Beaulieu where Armand lost his first game, won his second and third and made her play. Sara, following his lead won, They cashed their winnings, then left.

It was late when they returned to the hotel. She had

enjoyed herself, but felt relieved on reaching her room door that the need for pretence was over. She offered Armand her hand and thanked him for a pleasant evening. He held it closely. His dark eyes seemed to pierce through her reserve into her private thoughts.

'We must go to the skiing slopes again tomorrow. The championships are over and the snow will soon be gone. We must make the most of it. I will meet you in the hotel foyer at eight-fifteen. *Bien!*'

'Do you always get your own way?' she asked, trying to wriggle her hand free from his clasp in vain.

'Always,' he answered inexorably.

Deliberately he turned her hand palm upwards and kissed it. Sara's breath fluttered in her throat as he closed her hand gently and released it.

'Until tomorrow, *ma petite*. Goodnight.'

Sara slept fitfully that night, alarmed at the enormity of the task she had undertaken. Armand would not be easily fooled and he was so dangerously attractive. Whenever she thought of his kiss on her hand and his deep intent gaze lingering on her lips, she had the tingling sensation of his having kissed her mouth.

The rest of that week spent among the pristine peaks and blue-shadowed valleys in the mountains was something Sara never forgot. That magic top-of-the-world feeling, that sense of wellbeing in a wonderland of breathless beauty reached its peak on their last night after sleigh-bell rides, fondue parties and dancing to the music of zithers and brass bands.

To Sara it was the perfect end to a week of undreamed-of pleasures. Replete with a wonderful meal she sat with Patrice and Johan for the passing round of the Friendship Cup. It was prepared in a beautiful hand-carved wooden cup with four drinking spouts, one for each of them. Coffee with slices of orange was laced with strong white grape brandy, Grand Marnier liqueur and sugar. A match was applied and when the flames had died away the Friendship Cup was passed round for each one to partake of the heady drink. In a mountain inn at about five thousand feet up in the most glorious scenery they had all joined in songs, and beaming faces lit up the pine-walled room.

That last night Armand had accompanied Sara to her door in the hotel. Since the incident of kissing her hand, he had behaved impeccably, so his reaching out to draw her in his arms was totally unexpected. His kiss was warm and lingering. Sara, taken by surprise, gave herself up to the joy of it, hypnotized by the wild thrill hitting at every nerve centre. When sanity returned, she drew away from him, bade him good night and entering her room, closed the door decisively behind her. Her heartbeat had about gone back to normal when Patrice walked in.

Sara took one look at her happy face as she removed her make-up at the dressing table. 'Don't say it,' she teased. 'You're engaged.'

'I hope to be, with the parents' consent.' Patrice lifted slim arms above her head, then lowered them to hug herself. 'Isn't life wonderful when you're in love ? If anyone had told me a week ago that I should be looking forward to going home, I wouldn't have believed them.'

Sara used a face tissue. 'Then you're leaving this weekend as planned?'

'Yes. With Johan, of course. He wants you and Stewart to have dinner with us tomorrow night and go to a show. I want to thank you both for being so kind to me.'

'You've been kind to me, Patrice, in taking Stewart out of my way those first few days when I was feeling pretty low-spirited,' Sara stated dryly. 'How is he? I haven't seen him since you told me he had a cold.'

If Sara felt a twinge of guilt at not going to see Stewart, she dismissed it wisely. There had been nothing she could do in that direction without giving him the wrong impression as to her concern. He simply must be made to see that she wanted no kind of friendship with him. It was quite possible that he was aware of it by now and that booking in at the same hotel had availed him nothing as far as she was concerned. She hoped so.

Patrice had moved to the door. 'He's better and has agreed to go with us tomorrow night. I'm going to rush to

61

my room for something I forgot to bring. Shan't be a moment.'

She was back in no time with a small parcel which she placed on the dressing table. 'This is for you from Johan and me. We bought Stewart the same.'

Sara turned in her chair at the dressing table to look up at Patrice in surprise. 'A present for me? How sweet of you!' She smiled. 'I have one for you!' Opening a drawer in the dressing table, Sara drew out a packet wrapped in gay paper and tied with pink ribbon which she gave to Patrice.

'Thanks. Mind if I open it?'

'Not at all. I'm going to open mine.' Sara picked up her present and for a few seconds there was the rustle of paper. 'How nice!' she cried delightedly, gazing on a handsomely carved Friendship Cup. 'Thank you, Patrice.'

Patrice was equally pleased with her music box, which she opened. And as the tune of 'The Glass Mountain' tinkled gaily forth, Sara said, 'It seems we both had the same idea in mind, a memento of our skiing. It's been one of the happiest times of my life. I simply loved the warm comradeship and the funny oompah bands.'

'It's been the happiest time of my life too, because I met Johan again. I'll always be grateful to you for encouraging me to stay on at the hotel. I don't say I wouldn't have met Johan again had I gone home as Grandfather wished. But I might have met him again after he had married someone else. You see, he's now living in Berne and our paths might not have crossed for some time. We're hoping my parents will consent to us becoming engaged.'

'You like him very much, don't you, Patrice?'

'Yes, I do. And you – do you like Armand? I thought what a handsome couple you made, he so dark and you so fair.'

Sara coloured. 'He's been coaching me in skiing and I'm sure that's all there is to it – an ordinary holiday affair.'

Patrice grimaced in a nice way. 'And I was hoping you

would make a match of it. I'm sure he likes you. He has a good position and he's a wealthy man besides being a very handsome one.'

Sara replaced the Friendship Cup in its wrappings carefully. 'Like you, I shall have to fall in love before I marry. Money isn't everything, although it helps.'

Patrice nodded and closed the lid of the little music box. 'I agree. I'm glad that Johan comes from a wealthy family, though, because my parents might have withheld their consent to our engagement had he no prospects. His family are merchant bankers.'

When Patrice had gone Sara thought about Armand, finding it was becoming a habit. Far better to put him out of her mind until she had to meet him again. Maura had been terribly hurt by him and it was too easy for her to become painfully involved too. She was having an early breakfast in her room on Saturday morning, being uncertain about her plans for the day. Since her visits to the skiing slopes were ended she would have to set about enjoying herself on her own since Armand had not rung her room or contacted her about the day's activities.

Then the note came delivered by a hotel porter. She read, 'Sorry, I have been called away on urgent business and will be away several days. Look after yourself and think of me sometimes. Armand.'

Sara stared for deflated moments at the masculine handwriting and wondered why she should feel so shattered by his absence. It was the aftermath of a week of hilarious fun and games on the skiing slopes, of course. It could not be anything else, certainly not the man himself. Tearing her thoughts away from Armand, Sara remembered she was dining with Patrice and Johan that evening and began to think where she could spend the day. She had not made up her mind when, leaving her room, she met Michelle Despard coming towards her along the corridor.

Michelle was all smiles. 'Good morning, Miss Everette. I was on my way to see you to ask if you had made any plans for this afternoon. I have tickets for a fashion show in Nice and would be glad of your company if you are free. My husband has decided to take advantage of this glorious weather we are having and is spending the afternoon at the swimming pool.'

Instantly, Sara saw the invitation as a means of escape from Stewart. 'I'd love to go with you,' she replied without hesitation. There was something she liked about the Frenchwoman, even if she was a friend of Armand's. 'It's nice of you to ask me.'

Michelle put her arm through Sara's on their way to the lift. 'Pure selfishness on my part. I prefer my own company in small doses.'

Arriving on the ground floor, they parted, Michelle to join her husband waiting for her behind a newspaper in the hotel foyer and Sara to make her way outdoors.

At lunch time, Sara had already started on the main course when Stewart entered the hotel dining-room. His eyes lighted with satisfaction to see she was alone.

'Mind if I join you?' he asked. 'We're almost strangers these days.'

He took his seat opposite to her at the table and gave the waiter his order. Sara thought his face looked rather drawn and forced herself to be polite.

'I'm pleased to see you've recovered from your cold,' she assured him as he shook out his table napkin.

His reply was filled with acid. 'Awful places hotels to be in when you're ill. You appear to be enjoying yourself.'

The waiter brought his soup and Sara ordered coffee.

'Why shouldn't I?' she said. 'Do you object?'

He shrugged. 'I'd watch my step if I were you.'

Sara stiffened. 'I beg your pardon?'

'Don't get on your high horse with me,' he said infuriatingly. 'The window of my room overlooks the car park and I've seen you leaving in your boy-friend's car. I wouldn't get any ideas about him if I were you. The man is probably just amusing himself. You know, of course, that he belongs to the Romond de Poulain family and that also he is a technical adviser at the Quai d'Orsay in Paris.'

He picked up his soup spoon with some satisfaction. 'No chance there, Sara, of bringing him to heel. I would say he wasn't the marrying kind.'

The waiter brought her coffee and Sara was hard put to it not to throw it into Stewart's leering face.

'For someone who's been confined to their room you've been remarkably active. Did you employ a private detective?' she said sarcastically.

He shrugged his shoulders. 'I knew you wouldn't like me handing out advice. People never do. However, I did feel that some kind of warning was necessary in case you went off the deep end about him.'

A cold chill feathered across her skin. Was it possible for Stewart to be warning her about Armand because he knew of Maura's attachment for him? Yet how could he know? Maura had told no one but herself about Armand. How silly she was being. Stewart knew nothing. It was only a matter of sour grapes with him. He was jealous. Sara looked across the table into his cold eyes and a corner of her mind registered the fact that she had never seen them soften with any tenderness or feeling.

She said firmly, 'Your concern for me would be most touching if it were genuine. What I do, Stewart, is no concern of yours and never has been. I'm dining with Patrice and Johan this evening because it would hurt them if I refused. As far as I'm concerned, after this evening, you and I have never met.'

Her coffee untouched, Sara left the table feeling she would choke if she drank it. The hall porter accosted her as she crossed to the lift.

'Excuse me, Miss Everette,' he said, offering her a cellophane box containing an orchid. 'This came for you while you were at lunch.'

Sara thanked him and went up to her room. It was from Armand. He had written on the small card inside the box.

'Wear this with my love this evening. I want it to remind you of me. Armand.'

She put it in water in the bathroom. Stewart's jibe about Armand amusing himself came back as she got

65

ready to go to Nice with Michelle. In that moment Sara hated all men. And mixed with that hatred was the sweeter thought of revenge – revenge for Maura. The orchid confirmed Armand's interest in herself. If only she could make him care for her as Maura had cared for him. It would not be her fault if she did not.

Michelle, smart in a white suit, was waiting seated in her car. As Sara approached she opened the car door with an elegantly gloved hand.

'Missing Armand?' she asked, setting the car off and manipulating it expertly out on to the Corniche road.

Sara was immediately on the alert, wondering what exactly the position was between the Frenchwoman and Armand.

'You know he has been teaching me to ski?' she said lightly.

'Yes. Please call me Michelle.'

'Then you must call me Sara. Armand and I are only holiday companions.' She paused thoughtfully. 'Armand didn't by any chance ask you to include me in your outings, did he?'

Michelle chuckled. 'And if he did?'

Sara answered promptly, 'I wouldn't have come with you.'

Michelle sounded amused. 'Why not?'

'Because I know how little you see of your husband and I wouldn't dream of butting in between you.'

Michelle tossed her a brief glance. 'You won't do that. My husband and I are very close. He is a perfect lamb and spoils me horribly. Why do you think I came on this trip today? I came because I knew he would relax by that pool content in the knowledge that I was enjoying myself. As I've been at the hotel for some time waiting for him to join me, the poor dear assumes I am already bored with hotel life. Had I stayed with him this afternoon, Maurice would have enjoyed about an hour's rest by the pool before suggesting running me out some place to relieve my boredom.'

Sara gave a small sigh. 'How refreshing to find a happily married couple! There aren't many about these days.'

'Sounds as if you are a bit of a cynic where love and marriage are concerned. Are you?'

Sara laughed. 'Good heavens, no. I'm all for it.'

'Have you a fiancé back home?'

'No. But I'm not looking out for a husband. I'm on holiday.'

'That is usually the time when you meet him,' Michelle put in philosophically.

'On holiday?'

'No. When you are not looking.'

Sara shrugged, said flippantly, 'You could be right. I'll let you know if anything like that happens to me. Have you known Armand long?'

'Yes. He introduced me to my husband. It's a joke between us that he did it to be rid of me.'

Sara felt cold inside. 'Is that his usual line of escape?'

Michelle chuckled again. 'From his affairs? An attractive man like Armand is naturally on his toes and has to tread warily. I adore him.'

So Michelle was not saying. Pity he had not used the same discretion with Maura, Sara thought bitterly. Aloud she said, 'I think you made a wise choice with your husband. Being married to Amand would be like riding a tiger. You would have to be equipped for it.'

'But what a thrill! It would be up to his wife to learn how to handle him. I could have done it. But I fell in love with Maurice.'

Michelle went on to talk of the fashion show and a discussion on current fashions followed. The show was held at one of the exclusive hotels in Nice in an aura of plush-lined luxury. The decor of blue and silver was an ideal setting for the display of spring creations by a famous Paris fashion designer. On a delicate gilt-framed chair, Sara gazed at fabulous model clothes priced far beyond her means and thoroughly enjoyed it.

There was a short interval for refreshments and the

time passed pleasantly. Later, returning to the hotel, Sara thanked Michelle for a most enjoyable time and told her she was dining that evening with friends.

# CHAPTER FIVE

To Sara's surprise the evening with Patrice, Johan and
Stewart went without a hitch. Stewart, apart from a surreptitious glance at the orchid on Sara's dress, behaved
impeccably. In any case it was impossible not to bask in
the starry-eyed happiness of Patrice and her Johan. Sara
found him perfectly charming and very much in love.
After dinner, Johan had bought tickets for a show, a
sophisticated comedy by Feydeau which they all enjoyed.
The happy couple were leaving early the following morning and said their good-byes over a last drink in the hotel
bar. Sara was sorry to see Patrice go. She knew she would
miss her.

Both girls exchanged addresses, promising to keep in
touch. But Sara could not see herself accepting an invitation from Patrice to visit her in Switzerland. The visit
would recall memories best forgotten. In time to come the
memory of Armand and Maura would fade. It had to.
But a lot of water had to flow beneath the bridge before
that. She did urge Patrice and Johan to visit her in
London.

The next few days were spent in sightseeing, catching
buses to places of interest and filling every moment of
her day with activity. The beauty of her surroundings
seemed to add to Sara's unhappiness, for in her heart she
was dreading Armand's return. Hitherto, her thoughts
had been all of Julian and Maura. Now it was the man
responsible for her unhappiness who became the central
figure in her mind. His virile figure with his black dancing
eyes and deep enchanting voice with its alien intonation
strode through her dreams and gave her no peace.

Each day the orchid arrived in the little cellophane box
and she would brace herself for his return. Sometimes she
would positively ache for the time to pass swiftly to the
day when she returned home. Fortunately, there was
plenty to see and do, with frequent bus services to neigh-

bouring resorts.

On Tuesday Sara caught a bus to Vence. The weather had been fine, ideal days for outdoors. Sara liked Vence with its fine old gate ways and round picturesque squares where fountains played colourfully in the sun. After a visit to the eleventh-century cathedral, Sara went down the long hill to the village of St. Paul where she lunched at the Colombe d'Or. The terraced restaurant offered a splendid view of the surrounding country.

St. Paul was an ancient walled-in town. One entered by the north door on foot with the sensation of stepping back into the middle ages. The narrow streets, whose buildings oozed history from every stone, were a joy to explore. Walking around the ramparts with their enchanting views filled Sara with a sense of peace, transporting her back into those rare moments of time when one found a divine reason for being.

That evening, Sara returned to the hotel to receive the little cellophane box containing her orchid from the hotel receptionist. It had arrived while she had been out. Since Patrice had gone, she had not seen Stewart, and when he suddenly materialized beside her as she entered the dining-room for dinner that evening, Sara had the feeling he had been lying in wait for her.

'Good evening, Sara,' he said, with the smirk on his face she detested. 'Been out for the day?'

'Yes,' she replied coolly, seeing nothing else for it than to share a table with him.

His gaze lingered on her honey tan, the clearness of her dark blue eyes and the pale gold hair combed back from delicately blue-veined temples. Her lissom grace and demureness of expression fired his blood as no other woman had ever done. Sara, unaware of this, was being seated by Louis at their table; Louis, she thought, would probably have the impression that she wasted no time flitting from one man to the other.

The meal was punctuated by conversation, a little stiffly on her part. Stewart filled in the gaps by describing a visit to Gourdon, where from an altitude of twenty-five thousand feet, he had revelled in the views through bin-

70

oculars. He was surprised to learn that Sara had not been far away at Vence.

'Quite near to Gourdon. Don't know how we missed seeing each other. Did you go alone – or shouldn't one ask?' he inquired maliciously.

Sara decided to be flippant. 'Alone. The boy-friend is away.'

'So your romantic idyll is over. Hard luck, Sara. I doubt whether you'll see any more of him.' His small eyes strayed to the orchid pinned on her dress. 'Letting you down lightly, I see, with the little gift each day.' His thin lips curled with derision. 'You might be lucky. They could still arrive until you reach home.'

'I'll let you know, Stewart. You're so interested, I wouldn't dream of spoiling your fun,' she told him dryly.

Sara could not wait to get away, and directly the meal was over, she left him. Michelle and Maurice were entering the dining-room as she left it and they stopped for a short chat. Sara was pleased to see that Maurice had lost his strained look and was much better already. She refused their offer to join them after dinner, pleading tiredness after an exhausting day.

In her room, however, a strange restlessness seized her and she walked on to the balcony of her room. Leaning back against the window frame, Sara stood drinking in the beauty of the night, listening to the muted sound of the dance band coming from the ballroom down below. It was all so very romantic and one of those nights when anything could happen. The moon was rising to fill the heavens with a silvery light and gradually her tiredness fell from her like a cloak. Acting on a sudden impulse, Sara picked up her evening jacket and handbag and left the room, deciding to go for a walk.

Pushing up the collar of her evening jacket and thrusting her hands into her pockets, she walked through the hotel entrance, to collide with someone coming in.

Everything spun round her as Armand's iron grip on her arms whipped heat through her body, fanning it into flame. The black eyes were looking deeply into her own

71

startled blue ones and her practised approach was swept away along with her cool dignity as his deep voice reverberated in her heart like a gong.

'What a welcome, *ma chère reine*! Have you missed me so much, or is the kind hand of fate still pushing us into each other's arms?'

Sara answered breathlessly, 'Armand! I . . . I never expected to see you tonight.'

He glowed down at her darkly. 'Are you on your way to a date?'

'No. Just for a walk.'

Taking her chin, he tilted her face to search it. 'You have not been unhappy, *mignonne*?'

'Of course not.'

'Thought about me often?'

'I had no other choice, with your flowers arriving every day. Thank you for them. They were lovely.'

He laughed tenderly. 'Did you wear them?'

Sara opened her jacket to show the orchid pinned on her dress, and the glitter in his eyes made her drop her own suddenly.

'So you are going for a walk. Now you have a companion.'

Thankful that he had not kissed her, Sara allowed him to thrust his arm through her own as they went down the steps to the hotel. Her heart was still thumping away madly and it was quite useless to fight her obvious vulnerability at his nearness. Later, she would see the whole unhappy business sanely again. Right now, she could only give herself up to the madness of the moment.

At the foot of the steps, Sara paused as a thought occurred. 'If you've only just arrived, you must be feeling hungry and tired.'

'I had a meal in Nice.' Suddenly he was looking down at her, teasing and vital. 'Not trying to get rid of me, are you?'

'No, but I have had a rather full day and my walk will not be a very long one.'

'Then we will go for a run in the car,' he stated firmly, and lost no time in taking her to the car park. The spacious interior of the car held the warm atmosphere of him having just vacated it. Sara wondered how long he had been driving. Not that he looked tired. He sat back easily in his seat with his strong hands resting with deceptive lightness on the wheel.

As they sped along the lovely Corniche road ahead held a sudden magic. On one side the continuous range of mountains screened off the cold north winds and tempered them to a freshness of air which was seldom oppressive even in the high summer months along the coast.

It was Armand who broke the silence. 'Tell me what you have been doing while I have been away?' he demanded.

Sara related her experiences, the trip to Nice with Michelle, ending with her day at Vence.

'Ah, Vence. Did you see the little Gothic church there with all the treasures?'

'Yes. I saw the cathedral too.'

He shot her a swift glance. 'Ever been to Paris?'

Sara smiled. 'Yes, and Belgium and Germany, to compete in show-jumping.'

He was delighted. 'You ride?'

'I have done from a child.'

He smiled and gave her a brief appraising look. '*Bien*. We must do some riding. Are you not curious as to where we are going?'

'No. I leave it to you.'

'There is a hotel on the way to Cap d'Ail called the Estel, a select little place not far from the main road. It's a favourite of mine – beautiful grounds, a swimming pool and a beach. An ideal place for a honeymoon.' He grinned at her, his teeth white in the gloom. 'I thought a stroll down to the beach in the moonlight and then a quiet drink in the hotel afterwards.'

'Sounds enchanting,' she murmured.

He deliberately misunderstood. 'What does, the honeymoon or the stroll to the beach?'

'Let's try the stroll to the beach,' she said demurely.

He sped on, turning eventually between wide flung

gates up a drive and on to a parking space. To Sara everything about that evening was perfect – the Mediterranean dusk – the red-gold slice of sky along the horizon beneath the falling curtain of light – the soft whisper of fringed palm trees and the breathtaking beauty of the bay as they reached the beach. It was a red pool in the flame and gold of the sky in the setting sun. It was the climax to a day of discovery – the last of a series of breathtaking views which had kept Sara enthralled all day.

Armand had dropped his arm companionably across her slim shoulders as they stood silent on the edge of the water. In the haven of his arm, Sara, bewitched at the new and the strange, felt his masculine fragrance take possession of her inner self, to imprison her for all time. Far away on the horizon, the curtain of night fell lower over the golden glow and shut it from sight. Suddenly Sara shivered.

Instantly he was looking down at her with concern. 'Cold, *ma petite*?'

'No. Just someone walking over my grave – a saying we have.'

'You're tired and cold. Let's go back.'

They turned and walked back to the beautifully kept grounds with wooden seats placed strategically beneath trees and between flower beds.

They paused to listen to a bird in one of the trees and Armand drew her down on to a seat.

Sara sat enthralled by the liquid notes of the bird as her eyes searched for it among the foliage of the trees. She sighed, 'Beautiful, isn't it, here?'

'Ideal for a honeymoon?' he whispered above her ear as he lowered himself down beside her. His arm stealing around her sent warning tremors along her nerves. 'You know, *ma chère reine*, you are something I have never met before. Frenchwomen, on the whole, are eternally chic, congenitally feminine and coquettish with men in mind.' He touched her cheek with gentle fingers. 'You have a tantalizing untouched air, a freshness, a quality of delicate fragrance which owes nothing to artifice. In short, *mignonne*, I am mad about you.'

74

His voice, like his touch, was a caress. Sara struggled inwardly against an unfamiliar and exquisite emotion which was threatening to engulf her common sense. Her ultimate victory over a man who had wrecked her way of life was forgotten by his unexpected declaration. Shocked dismay looked at him from her wide-spaced blue eyes as he took her into his arms.

His lips rested on the side of her neck and moved up slowly to her mouth. In sudden panic, Sara pushed him away. 'It . . . it's getting late. Shall we go?'

'What you need, *ma petite*, is a drink to warm you up,' he drawled, releasing her immediately.

Somewhat confusedly, Sara allowed him to guide her into the hotel, seat her in a plush room and within minutes put a glass into her hand. She could not identify the nature of the drink, but she accepted it knowing he would insist on her having it. It ran through her veins like liquid fire, warming her through yet leaving her heart a dead thing in her breast. Away from his arms she began to think rationally. Was there a slight disappointment underlying the relief she had felt when he had let her go immediately on her protest? Where was the wolf who had broken Maura's heart? He was acting completely out of character to give in so docilely. Sara moved uneasily. What did she want? Was she so much under his spell as to forget what he had done to her dearest friend? They finished their drinks and returned to the car.

'Better?' he asked before setting the car in motion.

Sara replied politely in the affirmative, knowing that if she was right about him he would stop the car on their way back to the hotel at the first opportunity. He did. Turning off the road into a side one, he stopped the car and shut off the headlights. Then he turned deliberately to take her into his arms, determined this time to have his own way. It was not the slightest use struggling, for it was impossible to move an inch in his hold. His black head lowered and his mouth on her own was taking something from her that Sara felt would never be hers again.

After an eternity of time while her senses took off into orbit, he looked down into her face and smiled arrogantly. 'You're sweet and I love you. *Mon dieu*, how I love you!'

Then he was kissing her again, strongly, passionately, with Sara offering no resistance, only a passive surrender to the wild clamouring of her whole being. Making a desperate effort to bring common sense to her aid, Sara knew subconsciously that she was in danger of taking what he offered and so bring more unhappiness to herself. It was herself whom she feared, this stranger who only came palpitatingly to life in his arms.

She struggled, preparing to say cruel, cutting words, until a sane corner of her mind reminded her of her plan of revenge.

'Armand!' her gasp was a desperate one. 'It isn't necessary to go to all this trouble to keep me happy. I appreciate what you're doing, but I'm only on holiday.'

An eyebrow lifted rakishly. 'Is that why you held me off? Do you not know that the surest way to lead a man on is to repulse him?'

Her stare was one of bewilderment. 'But surely consent leads a man on more? What is a poor girl to do?'

Her innocent appeal brought the dark look back to his eyes. 'No problem there, *ma petite*. Marry the man.'

He met her startled upward glance with a hint of laughter in his eyes.

'On so short an acquaintance?' Sara was gasping like a fish out of water. 'You're asking for trouble!'

He grinned wickedly. 'But what beautiful trouble – to make love to someone you are crazy about for the rest of your life.'

Sara held him off desperately, afraid of taking the irrevocable step as she was aware of the strength of his light grip. 'Is this the line you take with all your women friends?'

'Hardly. I have never been married, and I have certainly never proposed to a woman before in my life.' He smiled down at her so tenderly that Sara lowered her eyes. Gently he drew her head against his shoulder and lowered his hard cheek against her soft one. 'Naturally this proposal from a man whom you know practically

76

nothing about scares you. I will not press you for an answer and try to contain myself for another week until you become used to the idea. During that week I shall do my best not to kick over the traces, but I make no promises.' He lifted her chin. 'You do like me a little, do you not?' Then, as she did not answer, he traced round her mouth with his own. 'Go on, tell me.'

'No. It isn't fair to ask me to say anything while under the influence of your lethal charm.'

'And is not your charm also lethal to me? *Mignonne*, you and I have something rare to give to one another – something that most people spend a lifetime searching for and never find. Is it any wonder that I want to make you mine in the only way possible by marrying you? I can never let you go now that I have found you.'

Sara never imagined he could be so humble, and although she knew victory was hers there was no elation in her heart, only a chill wind blowing over her.

They continued their journey between secret pine-covered hills, together yet miles apart with the ghost of Maura between them. The idea came to tell him the whole story of Maura's letters, her own suspicions, her agony of mind and the conviction that he was responsible for her friend's suicide. If he was guilty it was quite possible for him to lie. After all, she did not really know him.

Then they were turning into the drive of the hotel and he walked with her into the lift. At her door he held her hand as she thanked him for the drive.

'We are going skiing tomorrow before the snow goes. Be ready early.'

His eyes teased her – laughter lurked in their depths and she thought, I can see what Maura was up against, this congenital charm which made the blood run like fire through her veins. With her eyes on the dark vital face, she said, 'You might regret your kindness to a stranger.'

He laughed. 'The only thing I regret is having to leave you now.' And then, suddenly serious, 'I want to make love to you so much – to hold you in my arms and know that you are mine.' He lifted her chin with a lean finger, and bending his head placed his lips gently on her own. 'That is my seal of ownership. Let anyone who dares try to take you from me.'

Sara recalled his words later in her room. Her expression was empty, her eyes unhappy as she creamed her face before the dressing table mirror as she prepared for bed. It was a relief to know that Patrice would not come in at any moment for a chat, for she was too confused to think clearly. All she could think about was Armand's lips firm and demanding upon her own, and her own Judas reaction. It was ironical the way he had played into her hands, almost a laugh, had it not been so tragic. A shudder ran through her at the thought of him making love to Maura in the same devastating fashion. As she dwelled on this her anger mounted, brandishing a flaming sword of revenge against him. If she had wavered in his arms, she was firm enough now. She would be as ruthless and merciless with him as he had been with Maura.

The next morning Armand took her to the skiing slopes, and so began a time of breathless and exciting activity. They did everything – skating, ski-bobbing where they rode a bicycle on skis with mini-skis fitted to their feet, curling and pony-trekking. Game for anything, undaunted by spills and lack of experience, Sara took everything in her stride, her small face beneath the bright, bobbed woolly hat sparkling and enchanting. Armand's admiration for her courage knew no bounds. If he was in love with her before his love now was very apparent in his words and glances. In the excitement of so many thrilling pursuits, Sara forgot her intention to lure him on, little knowing that by being her own naturally tantalizing self she was succeeding in her plan far more.

The week went far too quickly, as happy times have a way of doing. On Friday morning they tobogganed down slopes, swerving around hair-raising bends at a terrific speed to overturn in a flurry of snow at the end, laughing and breathless. Over and over in the snow they rolled, to lie on their backs with helpless giggles. Armand rubbed his cold nose against Sara's snow-covered one, then

ou. How else would I have known what to look for
he woman who would make me forsake all others?
t enough to know that you are mine and that
and nobody will ever take you away?'

ulled her roughly into his arms, forcing her soft
to the will of his own. And Sara responded with a
ring heart. She wondered if he had gone this far
Maura and knew she could only wait and see how
really would go. She had to play her part.

ey were in the car on their last stage of the journey
to the hotel after leaving the helicopter on the
h. Sara sat quietly, with her hands folded demurely
r lap. Armand was as aware of her as she was of him.
looked fragile and he marvelled at the little core of
rage, the courage of a real little trouper, hidden in her
der frame. There had been times when she had picked
self up from spills before he could reach her, times
en he knew she had been severely shaken by a fall, yet
e had never complained. It had been in those moments
at he was sorely tempted to seize her in his arms and
ver her sparkling little face with kisses. There was a
ystery about her that added to her charm, and the
dness in her blue eyes stirred him as no other woman's
d ever done.

'Not mad at me for kissing you, are you, *chérie*?' he
asked, throwing her a tender glance.

Her voice was entirely expressionless. 'No.'

'You do not sound very convincing.'

'I suppose I'm tired,' she answered flatly.

He was puzzled by her behaviour, Sara knew, but not
half so puzzled as she was over herself. Had she no more
sense than to allow herself to become emotionally involved with him? I'm a fool, her good sense told her.
That devil-may-care handsome face of his has no truth
behind it.

Running the car into the parking ground, Armand
reached for her shoulders and turned her round to face
him. Firmly, a finger was placed under her chin and he
lowered his dark head. His nearness and the wild beating
of her heart shook her into submission. His kiss held no

hauled her to her feet, full of concern in case she was
hurt.

After lunch he suggested a walk up the slopes. 'You
don't have to be a skier to scale the heights,' he said.
'Walking in the snow-covered mountains can be one of
the most therapeutic pleasures in the world.'

Sara had never known anything so exhilarating. The
strong, thin, unpolluted air alerted her senses as they
walked up gentle slopes which were preludes to encircling
mountains. Higher up the sensation was magnified, revealing breathtaking views of the valley below while
overhead the white peaks loomed unconquered, poised
and ferocious and strangely beautiful in their mantle of
snow burnished to gold by the sun.

Armand held her hand firmly as they climbed. Sara
had learned about him during the last few days, discovering him to be loyal, generous in word and gift and
very considerate. Yet she felt she did not know him at all
– at least not the side of him that had done the cruel
things to Maura.

She recalled their spill in the snow that morning from
the toboggan, his black eyes glinting with devilment, his
hair tousled with the fringe of his eyelashes edged in
snow. Despite the lean hardness of his superb physique,
his wide-shouldered strength, he had been so boyish, so
endearing in a defenceless kind of way of being unaware
of her analytical regard. Sara felt again his firm cold
cheek pressed against her own and her heart lurched on a
sharp exquisite pain. Her thoughts became incoherent
whenever he touched her, something she had to learn to
overcome.

The muscles at the back of her legs began to pull, when
they reached a restaurant set high on a plateau. Armand
ordered hot mulled wine which he told her would combat
the cold temperature of the heights and looked at her
mockingly. Sara was not cold, her pulses raced and she
had never felt so fit. It showed in the brightness of her
eyes and her glowing cheeks which Armand surveyed
with an ironic appreciation.

'Enjoying it?' he asked, lighting a cigarette and leaning

back in his chair to blow out a line of smoke into the air.

'So much,' she answered, avoiding his narrow probing glance across the table.

Here on top of the world at a cosy table for two it was so easy to forget why she was there. And Armand, his gaze steady and preoccupied, wondered why those glorious blue eyes which seconds ago were so radiant and sparkling should suddenly become as cool as an English sky. That unhappy guarded look came back again when to all intents and purposes she seemed suddenly to have lost it.

They spent an hour in the sun before going on to the summit to board the cable car. Boarding it, they were carried above depthless ravines and gaunt faces of mountains on their way back to the skiing village. The evening was spent in the hotel by the lake, reached by horse sleigh to the jingle of bells. There they were entertained to a Tyrolean evening packed with folk music, dancing and traditional entertainment. Wine flowed, the waiters were run off their feet and music filled the air. In the centre of the polished floor a group of folk dancers in traditional costume whirled around, with the girls showing tantalizing glimpses of frothy underwear beneath the skirts of their embroidered dirndl dresses.

Later, Armand and Sara joined in the dancing. Candles cast a golden glow on pine walls, cigarette smoke curled upwards to the rafters and everyone was gay. Sara lost herself in Armand's arms as they glided smoothly around the room, moving as one. Thoughts of vengeance and the unhappy past held no place in the magic of the moment. If only it would go on for ever, this swooning bliss lost in a swaying rhythm of music in a place on top of the world.

Armand murmured, 'Tonight those blue eyes of yours are like stars, your little nose is tilted at the world in general, and your mouth—' He groaned. 'I cannot bear to look at your mouth without wanting to crush it beneath my own.'

He danced her on to the terrace and Sara took a deep

breath to give her courage. Then his lips claimed hers demanding terror, I've planned for this, but it the kissing, the physical contact ag little resistance. Her hands, instead were clinging and she was tremblin defences her conscience was offering.

When he slackened his hold to look those searching black eyes, she stared edly.

'Did I frighten you, *ma petite*?' he laughed exultantly at her wide-eyed would have drawn her closer. But his laug back into the realm of common sense. laced with shame brought a flush to he strength to her hand.

'You promised me a week,' she said, away.

'It is your own fault, *ma chère reine*, for b sirable,' he answered in a voice which was a steady for him. 'I want you so much.'

Sara held him off, hating herself for being no his lethal charm. Love to him was a game in w held the winning hand. The thought made her and she said bravely, 'Am I the first English you've kissed, Armand?'

It was a leading question. With bated breath waited for his answer, knowing he must surely reme Maura, who had loved him better than life. Would h her the truth? A surge of passionate hope whipped he a sudden breathlessness. The soft sweet night air was about them, moving the soft tendrils of hair against h temples. A pulse at the base of her throat beat as spas modically as her heart. Her eyes were dark blue pleading pools. Unconsciously, she put out a pleading hand as he remained silent. His eyes narrowed, travelling over her gravely.

'What do you want me to say? I have had affairs which have never meant anything to me at the time. But they do now, because they are a part of a chain of events leading

passion nor desire – neither did it frighten her in any way. It was a declaration of love from his heart, and Sara recognized it as such. But when he lifted his head the ghost of Maura was between them.

The foreign intonation in his voice was marked when he spoke. 'Sara, will you marry me, and soon?'

He had proposed! Sara, too shaken to answer, felt the colour leave her face, then rush back in a hot tide. She thought of Maura and her eyes filled with tears.

'Tears, *ma petite*? What is the matter? Surely you knew I loved you?'

'It can't be love. We hardly know each other,' she demured.

His lips brushed her own. 'It can be nothing else,' he insisted. 'Did I not say that the nicest things that happen in life are usually the most unexpected?'

Sara began to laugh. It was either that or cry. 'But you promised me a week's grace. Today is only Friday.'

'Which is all the time I am giving you, *chérie*. We are going to Paris to be married.' He lifted a hand when she would have spoken. 'I shall procure a special licence, your trousseau and everything will be taken care of.' He laughed, his teeth very white in the gloom. Sara felt like putty in his hands. Why did he have to be so overwhelmingly attractive? Why not more like Stewart, she thought despairingly, instead of a black-eyed piratical Frenchman? 'It's going to be wonderful,' he was saying. Then he was kissing her with a hard proud remoteness which began to fill her with a mixture of terror and foreboding.

'Please, Armand!'

Sara spoke against the pressure of his lips. But he refused to let her go, as if his very insistence would make her consent.

'Love me?' he asked, against her lips.

'I . . . I . . .' Sara could not go on.

Uneasily, she was aware of playing a double game involving a certain amount of deceit. For her own satisfaction she had to go through with it without lying if she could. It was enough to act a lie.

83

He laughed softly. 'Like me, then?'

'I can't help liking you . . .'

The words were uttered before Sara was aware of having spoken them. Triumphantly, he gathered her to him and ardent, breathless moments passed.

'Say you will marry me, *ma petite*,' he whispered at last urgently against her neck.

Desperately, Sara was realizing that the sooner she married him the sooner she would see the end to his love-making, which to her everlasting shame she was finding it harder and harder to resist.

'If you're sure you want to marry me, then I will.' She pushed him away. Her smile was piteous. 'No . . . no, don't touch me. Think it over. Tell me tomorrow.'

His impassioned look shook her, but she met his eyes steadily. 'Pack your cases tonight. I will see you in the hotel foyer at nine-thirty in the morning. And do not worry, I will take care of everything.' His smile was very gentle and he touched her hot cheek with the back of his hand caressingly. 'You are tired, *ma chérie*. You will feel better in the morning. Sleep well.'

To Sara's horror, her eyes filled with tears. 'Good night, Armand,' she murmured, and was out of the car before he could open his door.

# CHAPTER SIX

SARA, after a disturbed night during which she had little sleep, awakened to her own private torment. Ever since Maura's death she had thought bitterly of the man whom she held responsible. Now he had played into her hands, she was dithering about it. Was her love for her best friend so poor a thing as to make her want to back out at the last moment? She had to go through with it if only to gain a certain amount of peace and contentment. She could not face breakfast and ordered coffee, feeling the need of liquid to ease her dry throat. The hotel porter came for her cases at nine and she tipped him liberally. Getting ready to meet Armand was like preparing to meet a firing squad.

Armand was waiting in the foyer, smoking a cigarette which he put out immediately on seeing her. He took his time about looking her over, from the crown of pale gold hair and cream summer coat to the beige court shoes.

'Good morning, Sara, *ma petite*,' he said. 'Everything has been taken care of.' He took her arm and walked with her to the wide entrance of the hotel.

'And my room?' she asked as they went down the wide marble steps.

'Is yours until the end of the month. Surprised?' He smiled down at her wide questioning gaze.

'Yes,' she answered truthfully. 'Why?'

'Leaving your room free for the next two weeks will give you confidence in the way that I am not leaving you a leg to stand on.'

'You mean I have somewhere to run to if I get cold feet?' she asked in a voice which sounded hideously false and airy.

They had reached the foot of the steps and were making their way to the car park.

'I want you to be happy, *mignonne*.'

The black eyes bored down into her blue ones and she

85

managed a smile of sorts.

'I'm in a daze, but it's nice to know I can change my mind.'

'You have about two minutes.'

He helped her into the car as they reached it, striding round the bonnet to take his place beside her.

Sara sat very still, her fingers linked together in her lap as Armand slammed his car door shut, then turned to look down at her.

'I suppose the two minutes are up,' she said, lifting her eyes to his ardent look. 'I bet there never was any. You're a very persistent man.'

He laughed and took her in his arms. 'About time. . . .' he murmured, bending his head. Her lips were tremulously sweet beneath the pressure of his firm ones and his arms tightened. But after that one kiss he released her and started the car. It leapt to his bidding, the familiar circle was made and smoothly they slid out on to the road.

It was a dull, grey morning with a mist lying over the sea. Sara shivered although the car was warm. Something cold as steel encompassed her heart and she leaned back in her seat and closed her eyes.

Paris in the spring! Sara never forgot that week-end in Paris with the trees shedding their white and pink blossom like flakes of snow in the courtyards and street pavements. She was to stay at the town house of Michelle and Maurice Despard until she was married. It was in a select part of Paris tenanted mostly by professional people and reminded Sara of Kensington Palace with its mellowed stone architecture.

Armand drove into a courtyard of trees and colourful tubs of flowers and leaving the car rang the bell at one of the tall narrow doors. The barking of dogs accompanied by a woman's voice was heard and the door opened. The woman appeared to be in her forties, with somewhat enigmatic brown eyes and a rather sallow complexion. The two Cairn terriers jumping around her suddenly let out a cry and flung themselves on Armand in ecstatic welcome. He fondled them and introduced Madame Dubret, Michelle's housekeeper, to Sara.

Madame had evidently had her orders, for she received Sara graciously and led the way indoors after Armand had taken his leave to go to his chambers not far away. He was to return later to take Sara out to dinner.

Sara's room was light and airy with off-white walls, matching carpet and French period furniture. But Sara only saw it vaguely as she stood on the sea of carpet after Madame Dubret had left her feeling lost and troubled. An impending sense of doom settled on her like a cloud. Her mind these last few days was a confusion. She seemed to be imprisoned in some dark tunnel with no way out. The old familiar feeling of terror seized her – a terror which had begun on losing her father, her home and security. She had known it again on losing Maura and Julian. Then gradually the terror had fizzled out to a feeling of unhappiness. Would she feel better when she had taken her revenge on Armand? She would probably know peace of mind for a debt repaid. Happiness was a state of mind, finding joy in everything around you. And security? Could one ever find that in the world of today?

Sara gave a sigh of resignation and started to unpack her cases. She eyed her clothes critically, wondering how they would appear against the models of the set Armand moved in. Her evening dresses, all cut on simple classical lines, were above reproach. So were the two tailored suits for which she had paid more than she could really afford. They would have to suffice, for she had no intention of using any of Armand's money for a trousseau. In any case she would not need one. After the ceremony she was going to leave him flat.

The blue suit worn with white accessories would be ideal for the wedding. It suited her perfectly, deepening the blue of her eyes and, apart from white, was her colour. Sara was glad she would look the part of the sweet young bride. Her soft lips compressed, wondering where all the hate came from. It was an unfamiliar feeling, tinged with a conscience that burned. I ought to feel ashamed of myself for planning such a dastardly deed, she told herself wryly. And I am not. Once they were married she could tell him a few home truths. She only hoped he loved her as much as he seemed to do. She wanted to hurt him as much as he had hurt Maura. Sara closed the empty suitcases firmly and put them away.

She had dressed for dinner that evening when Madame Dubret came to tell her that Armand was waiting in the lounge. Madame was smiling; like women the world over, she loved a romance, and this lissom English girl was as sweet and untouched as a Botticelli angel in her white evening gown. As for Monsieur Armand, his black dancing eyes and splendid physique never failed to quicken her heartbeats and make her long to be young again.

Music was coming from the lounge, a piece by Chopin, haunting and beautiful. Sara entered the room aware of white and gold walls, rich drapes gleaming, the delicate outlines of well-preserved furniture, a baby grand piano, the well-shaped head of Armand outlined against the white wall. The room was lit with warmth and happiness and Sara was caught up in it against her will. She wanted to resist his appeal and could not.

Armand stopped playing immediately he became aware of her. He came forward with his clever brown hands outstretched, his black eyes dark with the look of a lover. Unhappily, Sara resented the fact that he looked more distinguished than ever, more poised and more arrogant. The more she came into contact with him the more she was enchanted. Everything about him, the deep sound of his voice, the turn of his head, his expressive black eyes, his courtesy and charm taunted her.

Allowing him to take her hands, she fought his magnetism for all she was worth.

'Is that look for me or Chopin?' he asked.

'I love Chopin. I've known him longer.'

The dark intent gaze narrowed. 'And me?'

Sara knew she was behaving outrageously. The odd thing was, she meant to.

She looked at his dark face, wondering if he would be angry and did not care. She was wielding the sword of vengeance and finding a vulnerable spot.

'Jealous?' she taunted impishly.

88

'What do you expect me to be?'

Armand made no attempt to touch her. He stood there having released her hands, his face expressionless. Was he hurt? Please let him be. He had hurt Maura so much, she thought. Pain clouded her eyes, but she forced a smile.

'Not of Chopin, surely?'

'Yes, *ma chérie*, of anyone who claims your love.'

'But you mustn't be. It frightens me, this . . . this power you give me to . . . hurt you.'

He looked at her keenly with those disconcertingly black eyes and he was all fire as he drew her into his arms. 'And to love, *ma petite*,' he murmured softly against her mouth. Ardent moments passed while he kissed her with a passionate intensity. The confusion sweeping over her was an all-consuming pain. She was inwardly resisting him even while her blood raced madly through her veins in a wild ecstasy. 'Do you know why you have this power you are so afraid of?' He spoke in the side of her neck as his lips moved up to her ear.

'Why?'

'Because we love each other.'

Sara wanted to shout, It isn't true. I hate you for what you did to my friend. Let me go! Yet she said none of these things. She was drenched in a sense of shock as she stared up at him bleakly.

He shook her gently. 'Sara, are you all right? You have gone as pale as a ghost. It knocked me sideways too when I knew how much I loved you.'

'Is that what it is?' she said almost inaudibly.

'Of course – which reminds me.' Holding her eyes with his, he drew a small box from his pocket and opened it to reveal a ring. Gently, he pushed it on to her finger, then kissed it. 'Like it?' he asked.

Sara swallowed on a dry throat, taken unawares. The diamonds sparkled mockingly at her wavering heart. 'It's beautiful,' she said, offering him her lips for the first time.

They were dining out and they set off in his car for a favourite place of his in Montparnasse. It was a mild spring evening. Trees were gay with blossom and flower-sellers abounded. Armand drove dangerously fast, like the rest of his countrymen, with a relaxed air exuding confidence. Cool sweet air played on Sara's hot face as they joined the stream of traffic flowing from the Boulevard St. Michel on to the Boulevard Raspail. But it did nothing to cool the eruption inside her. Why was she so chicken-hearted? After all, she was only doing what she believed was right. It was her duty to see it through to the bitter end. At last, bolstered by her own decision, Sara began to take an interest in her surroundings. There was the usual number of near-collisions one expected from a mixed bag of motorists, and Sara looked on with a mounting excitement. How she loved Paris with its cavalcade of history made famous by Danton, Victor Hugo and Alexandre Dumas.

The small inn Armand had chosen was neat, unpretentious and typically French. He parked the car beneath the plane trees and they were greeted by the maître d'hôtel, who ushered them like royalty to a corner table in the delightful panelled room. The meal was excellent, the courses many and varied, the wine perfect.

Armand teased her, touching his wine glass with hers, laughter in his dark eyes – laughter, mockery and provocation which never failed to move her. But by the time they reached the coffee stage Sara, replete with a good meal, felt better able to face him.

They drove back to Michelle's house beneath a velvet blue sky sprinkled with stars and there was no sound save the purr of the car as they sped through the night. It was strange, Sara mused, how well Armand and herself got on together. Not only did they share the same taste in things like sport, music, books and the arts, but they also enjoyed a quiet companionship – periods of silence when no words were needed – finding it sufficient to be in each other's company.

Sara had never been one for idle chatter. Rather was there a serenity about her, and certainly no maliciousness. Which was why she was finding the role she was playing doubly hard – this pain she was inflicting upon Armand to avenge her friend. But above all this was the potential danger of Armand – her vulnerability regarding his charm. She had to keep her head. Armand was no fool. He was a brilliant man with more than the average alertness. His love for her was a deep burning passion and Sara was afraid of the fires she had kindled burning beyond her control.

He left her at Michelle's door, refusing to go in. 'You have had a tiring day, *ma petite*. I have borrowed a riding outfit from a young friend of mine for you and it should arrive tomorrow. You are to be measured for one tomorrow. Sleep well, and dream of me.'

Those few days before her wedding gave Sara little time to think. They went riding together in the Bois de Boulogne, journeyed down the Seine in a *bateau mouche* among gay crowds of people, passing the Ile de la Cité and the splendour of the illuminated Notre Dame, visited art galleries, shows and night clubs, sometimes dancing until the early hours. The time went frighteningly quickly to Sara as each day was lived to the full. She loved Paris and hated to think she was spoiling the memory of it for all time by the revenge she was planning on Armand.

She delighted in their walks, with Armand's strong hand beneath her elbow as they explored the enchanting gardens of the Louvre and other places of interest.

They were poignant moments when Sara forgot her reason for being with Armand, moments when they had walked up the Champs Elysées to watch the whirlpool of traffic around the Arc de Triomphe.

'It's rather sad,' she murmured, gazing with a deep emotion at the flickering flame of remembrance. 'But it's inspiring too.'

Armand agreed, 'I find it so too. I hope you do not mind marrying a Frenchman, *mignonne*.'

Sara's only answer was to tighten her fingers around his own.

While she enjoyed her rides with him in the Bois de Boulogne, Sara could not entirely relax because of the opportunities it presented for endless times of intimacy. Armand was plainly delighted with her riding skill and he, of course, looked superb on his own mount, which he kept in Paris for his daily ride.

He was more disturbing, more arrogant than ever in his immaculate riding clothes, his love for her burning in his dark eyes, a love for which there would be no fulfilment. They had reached their usual stopping place where they dismounted to give the horses a rest before returning to the stables. Armand had dismounted first and had reached up to grip her small waist and swing her down, subjecting her to an almost brutal scrutiny.

Broodingly, he looked down at her, deliciously curved in the riding outfit.

'How do you manage to look so tantalizing yet still retain that maddening elusiveness that brings out the devil in me?' he growled savagely. 'Do you know, *chérie*, that I am doing you out of a grand wedding with all its trimmings in order to make you mine at the earliest possible moment?' His hands had not moved from her waist and he bent his head, his breath warm on her cold cheek. 'I am hoping that this way you have of keeping me out of reach is shyness.'

Beneath the trees with only the birds looking on, he drew her into his arms. His head came down, shutting out the world, the spell of his magnetism, the firm pressure of his lips robbing her of all coherent thought.

'Like me any better?' he murmured between ardent kisses.

'Sometimes.'

'Love me sometimes, too?'

There was an urgency in his mouth compelling her own to respond. Unable to answer, Sara pushed him away. 'Your ... your parents, Armand. What will they think about you marrying me?'

'You are marrying me, not my parents. They will adore you, *ma petite*. So will my man, Henri.'

'Your valet?'

'Who else? I must take you along to see my chambers.'

He did on the day before they were married. There she was introduced to Henri, who appeared to keep the place immaculate even to flowers in the lounge. He was a small, brown-haired, wiry little man who moved about swiftly and efficiently. He greeted Sara courteously and appraisingly, like a father vetoing his son's choice of a wife. She saw the devotion the man gave to Armand and her heart stirred. There was no reason for her reaction. It was the man's duty to look after his master. Valets were usually devoted to their employer. Why should she care?

Armand's chambers comprised two bedrooms with adjoining bathrooms, a lounge study, kitchen and dining-room. Henri served tea while Armand told her of his plans. As his parents were abroad on holiday, he asked Sara if she would mind going to the Chateau de Poulain for the start of their honeymoon. It would only be for about a week as he had to keep in touch with his office in Paris. Later, they could go away on a real honeymoon.

As for somewhere to live, there was a small villa in the grounds of his parents' estate which was ideal for them if Sara approved. And for a place in town, they could put up at his chambers until they found a suitable flat there in Paris. He knew most young things preferred city life. He did himself up to a point. His best horses were at the Chateau de Poulain, and some day he would have to take over the estate there. He had considered giving up his appointment at the French Foreign Office to take over a partnership with his father on the estate. His father had wanted it for a long time, but that lay in the future.

'Meanwhile,' he ended with a devilish glint in his eye, 'my bed here is big enough for two.'

Sara had listened and hardened her heart, thankful that it had not been necessary to furnish any accommodation for them. It would be easier to break away as things were. With luck, she would be out of it all by the time her holiday was over. Armand had given her a cheque book for her to buy whatever she would need regarding a trousseau or anything else. Sara did not intend to touch a penny.

She was aware of Armand speaking again. 'Michelle and Maurice are returning to Paris today and should be there when we go back to the house. They are giving a small celebration party for us tonight.'

Sara listened in dismay, realizing that he had heaps of friends in Paris who would be interested in his marriage. Surely she should be glad? The more public his marriage was the more humiliating it would be for him when she left him. She waited while he changed into evening dress and they went back together to Michelle's house. Several cars parked outside told them some guests had already arrived.

Armand, seeing Sara's rather hunted look, squeezed her arm as they entered to say compassionately, 'Only a few trusted friends, *chérie*. No one to be alarmed at.'

Michelle and Maurice met them in the hall to congratulate them on their engagement. Then Michelle took Sara aside.

'I'll come upstairs with you while you change, Sara,' she whispered. 'Unless you prefer to be on your own.'

But Sara was glad of the diversion. Time enough to think about tomorrow when she had to. They talked as she changed into the green chiffon evening gown. Michelle sat admiring the long silky pale gold hair twisted into a chignon on Sara's small head. She thought her small face seemed a little strained. It was only what one could expect when *la pauvre enfant* was getting married on the morrow with none of her own people there.

Michelle smiled rather anxiously. 'You have nothing to worry about in marrying Armand. He is very much in love with you. I have never known him to be so hard hit over a woman before. We are all so fond of him. I have known his family for years. You are a very lucky girl.'

Lucky! The word mocked. Maura had not been so lucky. Something stabbed at Sara's heart and she moistened lips suddenly gone dry.

'You don't think it strange he should marry an Englishwoman?' she asked warily. She tried to probe, took it casually.

'Not in the least. Armand is in love for the first time in his life – really in love, I mean. You need never be jealous of his past. Like every attractive man of means brimming over with virility and charm, he has had affairs. Yet he has never committed himself. He always said he would never marry until he found the one woman whom he would want to be tied to for the rest of his life.' Michelle's smile was easier. 'You must have had admirers yourself – which reminds me. Stewart Wilkes was very surprised to hear you had checked out of the hotel.'

Sara gave a start. She had forgotten Stewart Wilkes. Not that it was important. She only hoped she would forget Armand as easily when the time came to leave him. They went downstairs together with Sara, her face set in a conventional smile, wishing it was all over. The ordeal before her of meeting Armand's friends plus the strain of behaving like a happy bride-to-be brought a high colour to her soft cheeks and enhanced the deep blue of her eyes.

Armand was entranced at her appearance. He was talking to Michelle's husband and two other men when she entered. Murmuring something to them, he strode across to her with a look of stifled longing in his dark eyes and drew her forward to be introduced. Sara was vaguely aware of one or two distinguished-looking men and well-dressed women as she moved on among the murmur of voices like an incoming tide carrying her along unresisting to the final reckoning.

Sara sat down to dinner at a table gay with flower arrangements, crystal and silver candelabra. Armand was beside her and she viewed him dispassionately. I have to hate him, she thought. Even so, it doesn't prevent me from seeing how terribly attractive he is, as he still will be at forty, fifty and sixty, with his black eyes, his arrogance, and a charm so potent that the whole room seemed to be filled with it. Small wonder Maura was enslaved by him. The old familiar pain stabbed and, like memories, it lingered through the evening until she went to her room to seek forgetfulness in sleep.

# CHAPTER SEVEN

THEY were married the following morning. Sara had dressed in the blue suit with her heart dead within her. The sun shone lighting up the pretty room, but she scarcely noticed it as she drank coffee feverishly and ate nothing. Michelle came to her room with the inevitable something borrowed, something blue which happened to be a pretty lace handkerchief with her name embroidered in blue in one corner. She was a charming woman, Sara decided, and at the last moment was sorely tempted to confide in her. The moment passed when Madame Dubret came with a spray of orchids from Armand to pin on her suit.

It was over, and they were back again at Michelle's house for the wedding breakfast before they left for Armand's home. Sara smiled and talked with people to whom she had been introduced the previous evening and managed to behave like the conventional bride receiving kisses and good wishes graciously. At last the tinkle of champagne glasses, the good-natured raillery was over. The wedding presents which Sara had listed in order to send the usual thanks were left at Michelle's house to be collected later. They were on their way.

Armand stopped the car at the first opportunity to take her in his arms. This time he kissed her without reserve, forcing her lips to come to life beneath the pressure of his own. Everything he had felt for her, the most profound love, the irritating annoyance at the slowness of her response and the infinite pleasure of holding her in his arms, was in his kisses. And Sara, with disgust at her own bodily weakness, was carried along by his passion.

When at last he released her it was to draw a jewel case from his pocket.

'My wedding present to you, *mignonne*,' he said, snapping it open. 'I hope you like it.'

His look was tender as she gazed down on to a diamond

necklace and matching ear-rings on a bed of white satin with the name of a famous jeweller in Paris.

'They're beautiful!' she breathed, bemused by the fire of the stones. 'Only I wish you wouldn't do this. You're spoiling me, and I have nothing to give you in return.'

'You are giving me yourself, *mignonne*, and no one had a more precious, more enchanting gift. With my gift I give you my allegiance and all my love.' He smiled, looking strangely humble and not a bit like his usual self. 'You are not unhappy about something, are you, Sara?'

Her heart lurched. 'Why . . . why do you ask?'

The black eyes tried to hold her own, but she lowered her lashes. For a moment the silence between them was almost tangible. Then he said, slowly, carefully,

'Because apart from rare occasions there has been a reserve, a holding back, as if you are afraid of committing yourself.' They sat in another uncomfortable silence until he added, 'You are not afraid of me, are you, *chérie*?'

She eyed him covertly. He looked immensely fit yet strangely vulnerable, his eyes beneath the straight black brows broodingly dark. If she was afraid of him it was not for the reason he thought. Somewhat disconcerted and relieved that he had misunderstood her behaviour, she said lamely, 'Everything is so strange. Sometimes I have the feeling of having dreamed it all up.'

'It is no dream, my sweet, as you will discover when I really make love to you. You are everything I have ever wanted,' he said deeply, huskily, closing her fingers over the jewel case and bending his head to kiss her hands. He caressed them. 'Such small hands to hold my life's happiness, but no others would have sufficed.'

'That's where I have the advantage,' Sara replied, allowing the tension to ease between them. 'Yours are so much stronger and bigger to hold mine.'

'And I shall never let you go,' he stated forcibly. 'And now, about that dream. . . .'

It was the old arrogant Armand who proceeded to show her that it was no dream before he set the car in motion. Shakenly emerging from his kisses, Sara slipped the jewel case into her handbag, aware that the last few minutes had held a magic which was indeed a dream. It was the awakening she dreaded.

Sitting silently beside him, Sara watched the unfolding rich, lush landscape of the chateau country, the river's silver gleam on their left and on their right the cultivated fields and picturesque woods. Everywhere, spring had rejuvenated the countryside into a realm of breathtaking beauty. Sara took a steadying breath when after a long drive, Armand swung the car in between wrought iron gates standing open to receive them and drove along a magnificent drive. A sudden curve gave them a splendid view of the Chateau de Poulain.

Sara found herself staring in awe at a tall, classically built white stone elegant place with a magnificent roof and delicate spires thrusting their points into the sky. Possessions had never meant a great deal to Sara. She had never craved to be the chatelaine of a chateau or pictured herself the bride of a wealthy aristocrat. To know that she was both shook her profoundly.

'Here we are, Madame Romond de Poulain.'

Armand, grinning down at her, was about to open the car door when she laid a hand on his arm. 'Armand,' she whispered, her blue eyes taking in the family crest over the great arched entrance, 'is there a title too?'

He laughed. 'What are you whispering for? Yes, *chérie*. My father is the Comte Romond de Poulain. But do not worry, I shall not inherit for years. He is a very healthy fifty-eight.'

He had helped her from the car when she followed his frowning gaze. He was looking at a green car parked on the opposite side of the drive. The driver had evidently driven the car past the entrance to the chateau and turned it to face down the drive for a quick departure.

'*Le docteur*,' Armand murmured, as they walked up the marble steps to the door. A footman appeared promptly to Armand's peremptory ring on the bell.

'*Bonjour, monsieur, madame*,' he said suavely. 'Everything has been prepared.'

Armand smiled charmingly. '*Merci*, Raoul.' His arm was around Sara as the footman bowed them in. 'My wife, Sara. Sara, Raoul.'

Raoul, a thin austere fifty or so, greeted her courteously. '*Enchanté*, madame. May I take this opportunity of wishing you both every happiness?'

Armand answered for both of them. '*Merci*, Raoul. Surely that is Monsieur le Docteur's car outside on the drive. Is someone ill?'

Raoul looked grave. 'Monsieur le Comte' monsieur. The Comte and Comtesse arrived but an hour ago. It seems Monsieur le Comte picked up a bug while abroad and is very ill. The doctor is with him now. I informed the Comtesse that you were expected with your wife.'

Armand drew a hand across the back of his neck, a gesture which denoted his concern. 'Is my mother well?'

'Quite well, monsieur.'

They had entered a lofty hall bright and warmly lit by sunlight pushing fingers of coloured light through tall windows. A beautiful baroque staircase which, after the first dozen stairs, branched off into two into the upper regions, gave a dignity to panelled walls and crystal chandeliers.

A sudden movement on the right-hand staircase above them claimed their attention. A woman who had reached the small landing at the head of the last dozen stairs leading into the hall now came down eagerly, her hands outstretched in welcome.

She wore a high-necked long-sleeved dress in fine black wool and a jewelled brooch pinned near one shoulder flashed fire as she moved. Black court shoes accentuated the long slender legs as she hurried forward. Her brown hair, slightly streaked with grey, was coiffured back from her face and despite the obvious restraint on her emotions, her hazel eyes filled with tears.

'Armand,' she said huskily, offering him her cheek for his kiss. 'How happy I am to see you. Raoul has told you about your father?'

'Yes. What ails him exactly?'

'Some kind of foreign bug. Doctor Lacont seems to think he has the symptoms of it, a high temperature and bouts of unconsciousness. The doctor is with him now.'

'I will go to see him. Meanwhile,' Armand placed an arm around Sara, 'my wife, Sara. Sara, my mother.'

The Comtesse appeared to be aware of Sara for the first time and eyed her with frank curiosity which turned to open admiration. She stared at the blue model suit, the pale gold hair beneath the small white hat, the white column of her slim throat and the youthful charm of her slender figure.

Sara did not cling possessively to Armand's arm, staking her claim on him. Instead she moved forward with a smile, reluctant to hurt this beautiful poised mother of Armand's. Yet hurt her she must if she was to hurt her son.

'Welcome home, Sara,' she said warmly, taking her hand and kissing her cheek. '*Ma pauvre enfant*, your hand is cold.' Her own closed round it warmly. 'There is a fire in your room. I was surprised when Raoul told me about your marriage. Armand always said he would marry first and tell us afterwards.' She looked up at her son fondly. 'She is lovely, Armand. But you are naughty to have rushed Sara into it so quickly. I hope you will both be very happy.'

'Thank you.' Sara's voice sounded strange in her own ears. 'I'm sorry about the Comte. I hope he soon recovers.'

Her mother-in-law squeezed her hand before releasing it. 'I still cannot believe it. He has always been so healthy and strong.' Tears welled again in her eyes and she blinked them back determinedly. 'Take Sara to your rooms, Armand. I must see Cook.'

Armand put his arm around Sara as they walked upstairs. 'Still afraid?' he asked mockingly.

She answered with the warmth of his arm about her. 'Overwhelmed is more like it. Your mother is charming. It apparently runs in the family.'

'And you, *ma reine*, are adding to it.'

Armand escorted her up the left-hand staircase and along a carpeted corridor lit by tall windows. In their bedroom a log fire burned brightly. It was a charming room with a delicately tinted carpet, soft furnishings gleaming richly in the fire light and elegantly pretty furniture adding unmistakable character to the room.

Immediately Armand closed the door behind them, he took her into his arms. Sara felt the passion in him. 'Sara.' He spoke her name softly like music before he kissed her.

She thought exultantly, He loves me. And she was fiercely glad for Maura's sake. Her revenge would be all the sweeter. He left her after his impassioned embrace and Sara was thankful to be alone to collect her scattered wits. She was sorry about his father. As for the Chateau, it charmed her even while it told her she had no place there. She – Sara Everette who would never really be Madame Romond de Poulain – was an interloper.

She bent down to pick up the small white hat Armand had taken from her head and tossed aside when he had drawn her into his arms. He had tossed Maura aside as carelessly, as ruthlessly, she thought, biting her lip. How unfair that he should be so handsome – and his voice too. It should be harsh and rasping instead of like music. And his kisses sent a fire through her veins, setting little flames alight. What was he, a prince or a king of spades as black-hearted as Lucifer? If only she knew!

Sara dressed carefully for dinner that evening. Cécile, the maid, a small dark girl, had been in to unpack her cases. Sara would have preferred leaving them, taking out what clothes she would need for her short stay. A feeling of crisis quickened her heartbeats as the time for a showdown came nearer. Was she scared of Armand? He loved her, there was no doubt about that, and her admission that she had married him out of revenge would be a bitter pill for him to swallow. But she had to go through with it. She had to surmount all her difficulties. She would not be afraid.

But Sara could think of nothing else as she dressed for dinner that evening. Not long before the sound of masculine voices coming from beneath her window had drawn her across the room to look down on the driveway. Armand was walking with the doctor to his car. They had stood talking for several moments and both men had looked grave. She was sorry about the Comte's illness and her sympathy was with the Comtesse, whom she liked for her sincerity and warmth. Armand was very fond of his mother. His engaging smile had encompassed them both when he had introduced her, and although it had lingered more on herself, Sara knew the Comtesse and he were very close.

Sara chose the white evening dress, knowing Armand would want her to wear the necklace and ear-rings. For the first and last time, she thought bitterly, clasping the necklace around her throat. Their sparkle gave light and radiance to her pale face. Surveying herself, Sara gave a tremulous gasp. What a difference real jewels made! They seemed to add to her femininity and gave her an air of seductiveness. When she descended the staircase the Comtesse was already dressed for the evening and greeted her at the foot of the stairs.

Her dress of pale cinnamon brought out the lights in her brown hair and she looked sweet, Sara thought, but her eyes were red-rimmed as if she had been crying.

'You look beautiful, Sara,' she said with a warm smile. 'I'm afraid this is not much of a honeymoon for you, a poor start. However, Henri, Armand's man, will be sitting up with the Comte, so you will have your bridegroom for tonight. Armand will not hear of me sitting up with him, and you are not under any circumstances to be allowed into the room until we know what is actually wrong with my beloved husband.'

Slightly embarrassed, Sara bit her lip. She liked the Comtesse very much at that moment. She had shown not the slightest resentment against her. Sara knew it had taken tremendous courage on an adoring mother's part to see another woman take first place in her son's heart after it had been hers for so long.

'You are very kind,' she said sincerely. 'I am deeply sorry about the Baron's illness. Armand is here with you and I'm sure you have nothing to worry about. He will see that his father gets the best attention, and the Baron's record of good health should go a long way to pulling him through.'

The Comtesse looked at her through a mist of tears. 'How sweet you are, and how lucky we are to have you in the family. I cannot tell you what a comfort it is to have you here. I would have gone off my head if I had no one to talk to. Friends are not the same as family, are they?'

Looking back on her first evening at the Chateau, Sara saw it as a preparation for what was to follow. In the beautiful dining-room they were seated on high-backed chairs and were sipping aperitifs until Armand joined them. To take her mind off her husband, Sara told the Comtesse of her childhood, leading up to her visit to Monte Carlo and her meeting with Armand. And although she talked of her brother Julian and his post abroad, never once did she mention Maura. But Maura's presence was there when eventually Armand appeared looking dangerously handsome in evening dress with that charming smile that had so enchanted her friend.

He took his seat opposite Sara, kissing her in the warm hollow of her neck as he passed her chair to take the seat opposite to her at the table.

'I am having a specialist on tropical diseases to see Papa tomorrow,' he told his mother, who was seated at the head of the table. 'Meanwhile, the drugs the doctor is giving him seem to be having effect. His temperature is certainly going down.'

The Comtesse looked relieved at his words, but although the meal was excellently prepared and served, none of them did justice to it. Sara was only half aware of what she was eating and Armand, like his mother, ate sparingly. At the Comtesse's suggestion they had coffee by the log fire burning in the huge fireplace.

Armand was worried about his father, although he was very attentive to the two women. There was a dark look which made his face look sardonic in repose. Then he smiled at Sara and his black eyes both allured and startled, making her heart do crazy things. His mother drank her coffee and refused a second cup, saying she was going in to her husband to sit by him.

Sara, beside Armand on the gold-fringed sofa, accepted

another cup of coffee to moisten a throat gone suddenly dry. Numbly, she watched Armand's brown hands beneath the immaculate cuffs replenish her cup handing it to her with the utmost tenderness. They lingered over their coffee and he was watching the soft enchanting contours of her face in the firelight when she lifted her eyes to his. Their eyes collided and held, his hungering with passion. Holding her gaze captive, Armand put down his cup, then hers to place it beside it on the tray.

'*Ma reine*,' he whispered ardently, drawing her into his arms. 'I cannot believe you are mine at last and that this is our wedding night.'

He held her so tightly that Sara felt every bone in her body would be crushed as he was crushing her lips. His kiss was never-ending, drawing out her very heart from her body in spite of her inner resistance. When he released her lips Sara had never felt so shaken, so terrified in her life.

With his dark face very near her own she whispered desperately, 'Armand, I must talk to you. Please, let's go to our room.'

He looked down at her for a long moment with a dark questioning gaze. Then a smile lifted the corners of his mouth. 'You cannot want to go to our room more than I, *ma petite*,' he whispered.

On entering their room Sara walked to the fire burning brightly in the hearth. Although the room was warm she felt deadly cold. Then Armand was behind her, cupping her bust with his hands and kissing the side of her neck.

'Well, *chérie*, what is it you want to tell me – that you have several more husbands tucked away somewhere?' He sounded boyish and teasing. 'I hope you are going to say you could not wait another moment for me to make love to you.'

Sara went as stiff as a rod in his arms. Something of her antagonism got through to him. His hold became gentle. 'Was I wrong? Come, do not be afraid. I love you far too much to hurt you in any way. You know that.'

'I know it only too well,' she said flatly.

There was a pregnant silence broken by a log falling in

the grate sending up a shower of sparks. A French clock on the mantelpiece ticked loudly in Sara's ears. Slowly he turned her round to face him. Her face was so tragic in the flickering firelight that he said in concern, 'Are you all right? What is it?'

He dark blue eyes were the only colour in the face she raised to his.

'I'm not in love with you,' she told him coldly and clearly.

The fallen log in the fireplace was now burning brightly, filling the room with warm elusive shadows. Armand stood holding her loosely in his arms, drinking in her fairness, her eloquent eyes, her small face endowed with the power to stir him as no other woman had ever done. His love for her blazed in his dark eyes, giving her a wide-eyed frightened look which was her own undoing. He laughed exultantly and tightened his arms around her.

'You are teasing me. Sara, you lovely creature. Why are we wasting precious time?'

He covered her face with savage burning kisses, convinced that somewhere beneath her coolness and lissom grace there lay a passion equal to his own. His hand loosened the chignon of hair, which cascaded down on her shoulders.

Feeling bruised and battered, Sara wriggled free before he could bury his face in the silky mass of hair. He said nothing, only looked at her with all trace of the arrogant lover gone from his face. His expression was a mixture of puzzlement and concern. He lifted her chin with a firm finger and her hair fell in a shiny silken halo about her head.

His eyes had to be tender. '*Chérie*, what is it? You are not disappointed because we could not have a real honeymoon right away? I have to be on hand during the next few weeks on a matter of importance to do with the office.'

'Did you know I worked at the French Embassy in London?'

'But of course.'

She was startled. 'You knew? But how . . .?'

He smiled. 'I knew all about you. I even fixed it with London to make it unnecessary for you to go back and work out your notice.'

Sara gasped. 'You didn't? How dare you do that without my permission?'

Two perplexed lines appeared between the dark straight brows. '*Chérie*, you're my wife. Surely you did not think you could go on working there. What had you in mind? To commute daily between here and London?' He laughed. '*Ma pauvre enfant*, you are tired and overwrought. I have rushed you. I'll give you time if that is what you want.'

'I want nothing from you. Don't touch me!'

He stared at her in amazement. 'What is this?'

She moved behind a chair to clutch the back with a grip showing white knuckles.

'Do you remember a girl named Maura Penhurst who came to work at the British Embassy in Paris last year?'

He frowned and moved a hand over his clean-shaven chin. 'Maura Penhurst? The name is familiar. Ah!' He clicked his fingers together in the air. 'I have it. Was she not that poor child who died from a dose of sleeping pills?'

He lifted a charming brow and Sara hardened her heart. 'So you remember her? How kind of you!'

He was puzzled, she could see. 'What has she to do with us?'

Sara, trembling a little, said laconically, 'Everything.'

Armand looked at her uncomprehendingly. 'In what way?'

She pulled herself together and stared at him coldly. 'You don't remember?' she asked incredulously.

Armand was frowning heavily. 'Remember what?'

'That you had an affair with her – that you led her on so much that in the end she had no wish to face life without you. So she took the only way out. How hard, how cruel you were. I wonder how many more women you have broken by your charms and forgotten them as you have Maura?'

Sara spoke with contempt, her eyes on his enigmatic dark intent face, and she saw him go pale.

'The girl's death was an accident, surely. Did she not take the sleeping pills after consuming an amount of alcohol at a party?'

'Yes, a party at the Embassy. I have Maura's last letter which she wrote to me before she died. In it she said she was hoping to get over her love for you. She was filled with despair and said she would rather die than leave you. She did.'

Armand gave her a startled look, but her eyes did not falter from his. 'Because of me?' His surprise seemed genuine, but Sara refused to be impressed. She watched his dark eyes narrow down at her. 'Sure you are not confusing me with someone else?'

'No. She told me all about you – your parties, your midnight bathing, the rides in your car. You really went to town, didn't you? What are you, Armand, two men?'

'At the moment I seem to be only one – a blackguard, a seducer of women.' He made a gesture with a lean brown hand. 'You believe this vile thing of me, your husband whom you professed to love, honour and cherish?'

'I never loved you.'

He stared down at her then, his eyes hardening, looking her over, his face a hard mask. 'What are you trying to tell me?'

'That I don't love you. How could you expect me to love the betrayer of my best friend?'

For palpitating moments they measured glances like sworn enemies. Then, with a smothered exclamation, he swept the chair out of her trembling grasp and took her by the shoulders. His grip was excruciating. 'You cannot believe this thing of me. You are tired, *ma petite*, disappointed at not having a honeymoon.'

'Honeymoon?' All the contempt she was capable of was in the word. 'Honeymoon?' she repeated as if it was a dirty word. 'Do you imagine for one moment that I would want a honeymoon with you, that I would allow you to make love to me – you – my friend's betrayer?'

'But you have let me make love to you?'

'Yes, and every time your lips touched mine I've shuddered inwardly, remembering that once they touched Maura's. Do you think I'll ever forget that?'

He gave her a proud astonished look, the black eyes blazed, but his voice was controlled and ominously low. 'Why on earth did you pretend to love me? Why marry me when you hated me so much?'

He was looking at her with a proud and savage anger as if she were some stranger and she was conscious of a searing pain around her heart. Tears tore at her throat, but she said firmly, 'I married you to avenge a friend who was like a sister to me. I married you because I knew you wanted me as Maura wanted you. I'm spurning you now as you spurned Maura. All your life you have had the best of both worlds – an inheritance, wealth, social position, a successful career and affairs with women. Well, Armand, even you have to know failure once in a while. You're getting off lightly for what you did for Maura. I know your feelings can't run very deeply, but I hope you love me as much as Maura loved you, because you will never possess me. Never!'

He let her go then, drew a case from his pocket and lit a cigarette. Dragging his gaze from the glowing end, he looked at her slightly dazed. 'And where do we go from here?'

Something in his tone, a momentary bewilderment overlying all his arrogance, touched her then. She knew she had hurt him desperately and completely. Maura was indeed avenged. Yet she felt no triumph, only a confused pain somewhere inside her which deepened every moment at the desolation on his face. And suddenly her desire for revenge was no more. The flaming sword she had been using clattered at her feet. Her elation turned to revulsion at herself and the role she had played.

'I shall be leaving when I've packed my cases,' she said in a voice she hardly recognized as her own.

'Are you? I think not.' He blew a ring of smoke into the air and again he was the old insolent, arrogant Armand she had first met. He towered above her larger than life.

'So far, *ma petite*, you have been the piper who called the tune. Now it is my turn. Why did you not tell me while we were in Paris all this ... fairy tale you believed, this distortion of the facts? Am I not to be allowed a word to say in my defence?'

'If you have an explanation, I shall be glad to hear it.'

Sara spoke flatly in an expressionless voice. There could be no possible explanation, yet she longed to think there might be.

He strode to an ash tray on a nearby table and crushed out his cigarette with unnecessary force. 'Like hell you would,' he said savagely. 'And do you think I would give you that satisfaction? I might have done so had you said you loved me in spite of what you believed about me. But you have never loved me. You hate me. So there is no point in saying anything. I see now why you did not say anything about it in Paris.' He looked at her broodingly, his eyes full of contempt. 'Like Shylock, you wanted your full pound of flesh — not only to make a fool of me in the eyes of my friends but also my parents.' He thrust his hands into his pockets angrily and walking to the fireplace turned round to face her.

In the flickering light of the fire, his face bore a haggard look and her heart, swelled with emotion. Sara was utterly bewildered by this new feeling — the inexplicable longing to touch his face. He was like a man who craved action when action was denied. She was wishing she was miles away, wishing she might have been spared to witness his hurt. Yet the hurt to his shallow feelings would only be temporary. He had probably loved her because she had been unattainable, a challenge to his power over women. She tried not to wince at the gleam of derisive resignation in his eyes. The king of spades indeed!

When he spoke again every word flicked her like a whip on a raw wound. He was savagely angry, his mouth a mocking, twisting thing. 'I am trying to believe all that you have told me and I am finding it devilishly hard to alter my former opinion of you. I would have staked my life on your honesty and integrity. To me you always seemed so vulnerable to life and its problems, and I adored your sweet gay humour, your courage to accept a challenge, rather like myself. But that was not the real you, was it? It was all part of an act put on for my benefit,' sarcastically, 'or should I have said my downfall?' He looked her over like a careful insult as though comparing her with his former conception of her. His eyes narrowed cruelly. 'Even so, you are not having things all your own way. You shall not leave this chateau until I say so. My father is very ill, he might even die.' A muscle moved in his cheek, but his expression did not alter. 'My mother will need female companionship during the ordeal she has to face.' He smiled unpleasantly. 'Strange that she too should be taken in by you. She thinks you are sweet and absolutely adorable.'

Sara lifted her chin militantly. 'And if I refuse?'

'I do not think you will. I am appealing to that faint little streak of decency which is said to lie dormant in even the worst of us.' Sara winced and he went on. 'My parents worship each other, have done all their married life. You could not begin to understand that. What do you know of love, much less the kind which sends one person barefoot if need be across the world to be with the beloved?'

Sara recoiled from the biting savagery, his contempt hurting her worse than the actual words. While he was strong enough to face the biggest odds even he was baulked by sickness. If he was comparing his conception of her with the one he believed to be the right one, so was she. Was it possible for her to be wrong? Treating Maura as he had done was completely out of character with the angry, disillusioned man now facing her. Then why had he not told her what had really happened to drive a happy-go-lucky girl like Maura to her death? Was it pride? Or was he guilty and realized his folly too late to make amends? Perhaps he had been trying to do so in marrying another English girl – herself.

Explanations ran around in her mind like a demented hornet imprisoned in a glass bowl. 'I'll stay,' she said. 'But not until you tell me to go. I'll stay to help your mother and I shall go when it suits me.' She swallowed, and although the words seemed to stick in her throat, she spoke the truth. 'I am very fond of your mother and I'm deeply sorry to hurt her in any way. Furthermore, I don't regard your request as being kind to her. Better for me to go now before she becomes too attached to me than later. If I go now she'll soon get over it and forget the whole affair, because she's too concerned with your father at the moment for anything else to really register.'

'I will take full responsibility for that. I have your passport, in any case. If you remember, I did not return it to you on the night you produced it to enter the casino.' He gave a bitter laugh. 'I hung on to it with the feeling that the possession of it brought you nearer to me, made you more mine. Love makes fools of us all, it seems.'

The sound of the communicating door closing after him held a decisive click, rather giving him the last word. Alone in the elegantly furnished room, Sara wondered if, had she seen the result of her vengeance beforehand, she would have gone through with it. It was something she had not foreseen, this humiliation at Armand's hands. In fact she was not sure whether the victory was his. He had conducted himself with admirable self-restraint and the look of contempt he had favoured her with rankled. Furthermore, he had only insisted upon her remaining under his roof until such time as his mother would be over the worst of her trouble.

Sara drifted through the drill of preparing for bed trying to find that contentment her revenge on Armand was going to bring her. Sleep was a long time in coming as she tossed and turned, ever aware of the set of masculine brushes on the small table near her bed. The sunlight was well into her room when she awoke the next morning, and the first thing she noticed was that the brushes had gone. At what time had Armand come in her room to fetch them? Her face went hot at the thought. All was silent in the room except for the ticking of the French clock on the mantelpiece. There was no way of knowing if Armand was in the next room. He had a second door leading from his rooms on to the corridor and he could have used that to go downstairs.

Sara trembled at the thought of meeting him again and she dressed leisurely, hoping that the Comtesse would be down to breakfast when she was ready to go downstairs. She was reading her mail when Sara entered the room. There was no sign of Armand.

'*Bonjour*, Sara. You are just in time for fresh coffee. Raoul is bringing it. Ah, here he is.'

The footman entered as she spoke with a tray and Sara sat down at the table with relief. 'How is the Comte?' she asked.

'No change.' The Comtesse passed Sara her coffee, smiling bravely. 'I pray there is better news when the specialist has been to see him.' She poured herself a cup of coffee and stirred in the sugar thoughtfully. 'Armand suggested I take you around the Chateau this morning, but I insisted upon him taking you round the stables himself. He took over from Henri this morning at four to sit by his father. Henri will take him off at ten for Armand to have a wash and breakfast. The specialist is expected at noon, so there will be ample time for Armand to take you round the stables before the great man arrives.' She laughed. 'Here am I telling you this when Armand has already done so.'

Sara buttered a croissant. 'It's sweet of you to tell me in any case,' she stated firmly. 'After all, I'm practically a stranger to you, yet you've made me feel as if I'd been here for years. You've accepted me so warmly, so sincerely.' To her dismay the tears rose in her eyes.

'And why should I not? You have brought happiness to my son and that happiness comes also to me. My only worry is will you enjoy the country? Most young people resent being buried in the country and prefer life in the city. You will have your own place here, of course, and will not have to live in with your in-laws.' She smiled speaking urgently and hurriedly with a need to reassure. 'The Petit Chateau is enchanting and just far enough away from here to be private for you. The eldest son of the family has always gone to live there on his marriage. Armand must take you round it. It is fully furnished and fires are put in the rooms once a week to keep it aired. Do you like the country, Sara?'

Sara replied spontaneously, 'I love it.' She smiled, responding to the Comtesse's warmth like a flower to the sun. 'Has Armand told you I ride?'

'No. Armand is very reserved and keeps most of his business to himself, although he will probably confide in you. He loves you very much.'

He did, Sara thought wryly.

Her tour of the Chateau later, with Armand's mother treating her like one of the family, was something Sara enjoyed. She looked about her with lively interest. The grandeur of the high-ceilinged, panelled rooms with their rich furnishings and *objets d'art* were mute testimony to the ancient lineage and history of the family. Nowhere was the atmosphere or decor ever sombre. Each room was filled with a warm golden light which blended the modern lines of the few contemporary pieces of furniture into the antique without detracting from it.

They arrived back in the hall to see the footman taking delivery of several parcels from a post office van at the door. Sara stood by while the Comtesse scrutinized them before giving her a large square cardboard box.

'For you, *chérie*,' she said.

Sara took it up to her room and opened it to find a riding outfit. It was beautifully made and fitted her perfectly. To her surprise the soft hand-made leather riding boots fitted also. As Armand was to show her round the stables she decided to leave it on, adding a yellow sweater in soft fine wool which suited her pale honey tan and brought out the lights in her pale golden hair. Surveying her reflection in the dressing-table mirror, she felt no elation at her smart appearance and went downstairs, preparing herself for a meeting with her husband.

She was aware of him immediately she entered the room. He was standing at a table pouring coffee from a silver percolator. He lifted his dark head as she entered, and Sara, impelled by some unseen force, lifted her eyes to look at him across the room. The next moment their eyes collided with a queer electric shock on her part.

Armand appeared unconscious of it, for he greeted her

coolly, enigmatically.

'*Bonjour*, Sara,' he said evenly, his black eyes flickering over her shapeliness impersonally. 'I trust you slept well?'

'Yes, thank you,' she replied, then realized it was a lie. She looked round nervously for his mother.

His expression became faintly mocking. 'Mother will not be joining us for coffee. Do sit down. I believe you have been on a tour of the Chateau.'

Sara sat down on the edge of a chair and he passed her a cup of coffee.

'Thanks. Yes, I have,' she answered. Unlike herself he was complete master of the situation, putting her at a disadvantage by his icy calm. Was it possible that her revenge had misfired and gone off like a damp squib? There was no hint of any disillusionment on his face this morning. True, he had used her name instead of the usual endearments to which she had grown accustomed and his eyes were hard and cold, which was what she could expect. He was also keeping his distance in a situation that would be intolerable had he insisted upon his rights as a husband.

He leaned back against the table to drink his coffee. 'What do you think about it?' he asked politely.

'About what?' Sara stared down into her coffee.

'The Chateau, of course. What did you think I meant?'

'The riding clothes.'

'Ah, yes. Do they fit comfortably?'

'Yes, thank you. I like it very much.'

He slanted a mocking glance at the delightful picture she made as a truant beam of sun sprayed gold dust on her hair, enhancing the peach bloom of her skin and the blue jewels of her eyes.

'I would say the outfit likes you too. You certainly go well together.'

No endearments, not even mocking ones. Sara wondered why she cared. 'The Chateau was rather a surprise,' she said.

'Indeed? In what way?' An eyebrow raised carelessly.

114

'Did you expect drawbridges and smelly moats?'

'I never thought about them. No. I expected a certain mustiness and the usual dark dank rooms one finds in many very old buildings. But this has none. There doesn't seem to be any skeletons in the cupboard of any of the rooms. There is a kind of glowing warmth about them. Everything is so well preserved with a kind of youthful mellowness.'

'For which my parents are responsible. My father loves his life as a country squire. I believe that is the term you would use. His day begins at six in the morning until any time in the evening before dusk. The estate comprises thousands of acres of farmland, farms and cottages and my father puts in more time than the people he employs. He likes it that way. You have not met him yet because the nature of his illness is not yet known. Mother appears to be immune to it, which is why she is allowed to sit by him.'

Her approval of the Chateau seemed to have softened him a little, but now he seemed to clam up all at once, speaking almost curtly when Sara said she hoped he would soon be well again.

'We can only live in hope. Come, I will show you round the stables.'

He put down his cup and Sara followed suit, leaving most of her coffee. The wall of reserve falling between them was an impenetrable one. If his mother had done her utmost to draw her daughter-in-law into the family circle, her son was doing his utmost to keep her out.

Armand strode to the door, opened it and allowed her to precede him across the hall. Sara walked beside him out into the brilliant sunshine; with her riding breeches smoothly fitting her neat hips and her back straight, there was a kind of dignity about her, a withdrawn untouchable air. The graceful sweep of her pale gold hair suggested a natural controlled beauty that was characteristic of everything about her. Yet she was anything but controlled inside. Armand did not speak and to Sara the silence became unbearable.

'While I appreciate the riding outfit, it hardly seems

worth buying for the short time I shall be here,' she said for want of something to say.

'Keep it as a souvenir of a marriage that never was,' he answered dryly. 'An annulment will be easy to obtain.'

Sara flushed at his tone. Here again was the old insolent man she had taught herself to hate. 'Just like that,' she remarked flippantly. 'Your friends will be surprised.'

He was unperturbed. 'On the contrary, everyone will understand. Who wants a frigid wife anyway?'

Sara saw a fly-past of the last tormenting months and she bristled. 'Don't congratulate yourself too soon. I could make the suit drag on by saying I hadn't actually refused to consummate the marriage.'

Sara flushed deeply at her own daring, appalled by the little imp of perversity urging her to war with him. Her heartbeats quickened as she gave him a hostile look.

Surprise darkened his eyes into quizzical disbelief. 'Take care,' he warned, 'I could take you up on that.' His shrug was negligible. 'Too bad I am no longer interested.' His brooding look became savagely cruel. He was intent upon hurting her. 'Could the fact of your not being a virgin inspire that last dangerous remark?'

Had he struck her, Sara could not have gone paler. Her lips felt as colourless as her face. But her air of youthful dignity was touching. 'You judge everyone else by your own standards, so your opinion of others is bound to be a little warped. At last you're running true to form. As for belonging to you – I'd rather die!'

The sudden gleam in his eyes sent a quiver along her spine as reckless, tearing anger gave her strength. He was angry. It was there in the thinness of his mouth and the jutting of his jaw, yet he exercised remarkable self-restraint. Each word he uttered was guaranteed to find its target.

'At least you are honest regarding your feelings for me. However, I would advise you not to remind me too often of them. I might take a sadistic delight in forcing my attentions upon you just for the thrill of watching you recoil in horror. In any case, a certain amount of petting will be necessary between us.'

Sara's voice was a low husky whisper. 'What do you mean?'

'Surely you know we shall have to keep up appearances when in public. We are supposed to be on our honeymoon, and this is where it begins, so smile and look happy – and remember, it is just as distasteful for me as for you.'

He had put his arm around her trembling figure as they entered the stable yard where a groom was filling a pail with water from a pump. He put down the pail on seeing them and strode towards them.

'*Bonjour*, monsieur, madame,' he said respectfully.

'*Bonjour*, Jean-Paul,' Armand answered smoothly with his charming smile. 'Sara, this is Jean-Paul, our head groom. Jean-Paul, my wife Sara.'

'*Enchanté*, madame,' Jean-Paul greeted her courteously with a look of appraisal. 'May I be permitted to wish you both every happiness?'

Armand answered for them both. '*Merci*, Jean-Paul. Has Madame's mount arrived?'

'This morning, monsieur, and she is in fine fettle.'

She was in the first stall, a beautiful chestnut with a coat like satin.

Sara gave a cry of delight and fondled the silky neck. 'What a darling,' she exclaimed. 'What is her name?'

'Mimi, madame.'

Jean-Paul stood by with the manner of a proud parent. Small of stature and wiry, he gave the impression of having been a jockey in his youth. His thin brown face and grey hair put his age around fifty.

Armand's hand touched Sara's as she drew it down the horse's neck and her own tingled from the contact. If he saw her sudden withdrawal, he gave no sign. He addressed Jean-Paul in a deep grave voice.

'Will you accompany Madame on her first ride, Jean-Paul? Show her the landmarks and boundaries. I have to remain within call.'

'*Oui*, monsieur.'

Jean-Paul went to put on Mimi's saddle while Sara

waited for Armand to speak. She knew he had plenty of time to accompany her for an hour's ride, at least, and she felt snubbed. In any case he had no intention of accompanying her since he had not put on his riding things. An ice-cold feeling drenched her from head to toe. Why had she not left as she had planned instead of staying under such ridiculous conditions? The answer was there in a sensible little corner of her mind. While she had to inevitably inflict hurt upon the Comtesse through her son there had to be a humane way of doing it by putting her into a condition for receiving that hurt. She was certainly in no condition at the moment for extra cares.

Still no comment from Armand to fill in the breach until Jean-Paul brought the horses. She was aware of his fine dark features, his handsome leanness and that glass-topped wall between them, impenetrable as a fortress.

When Jean-Paul came leading the two horses, Sara met him eagerly, mounting Mimi before Armand could assist her. Then Jean-Paul joined her and they trotted off together. Armand stared after the two riders and his face was set in weary, bitter lines. It was some time before he went back indoors.

# CHAPTER EIGHT

SARA saw the specialist arrive when she returned from her ride with Jean-Paul. He was a tall, lynx-eyed man, middle-aged and slightly bald with a proud carriage. He was inclined to be optimistic over the Comte's illness when he joined them at lunch. He had diagnosed a kind of sleeping sickness and he wanted the Comte removed at once to hospital in Paris for immediate tests and treatment.

Armand and his mother agreed for the Comte to go, and lunch was a pleasant meal with the cloud of depression brought on by the Comte's illness finally lifting a little. The specialist, Monsieur Ravel, proved an excellent raconteur and Sara laughed often at his wit. He made no secret of his admiration for her and they all laughed when he asked if she had any sisters.

For the sake of appearances, Armand addressed her from time to time with small endearments, but the tender words were contradicted by the mocking derisive gleam in his eyes and the cynical curve of his mouth.

After lunch, Sara packed a bag on the Comtesse's instructions. They were to follow the ambulance taking the Comte to hospital in Armand's car. But before the ambulance arrived, Armand's mother collapsed in her room. The little maid came running to tell Sara who was just in time to see Armand carrying his mother's still form to the bed. Monsieur Ravel was there, lifting an eyelid of the Comtesse's ashen face while Armand looked on anxiously.

The minutes ticked by with Sara watching Armand unobserved, so intent was he on that still figure on the bed. One brown hand sought the back of his neck to rub it unconsciously – an action Sara found oddly defenceless, like that of a small boy despite his height and breadth of shoulder. His thick dark hair was ruffled, his mouth tightly set – the mouth of a man who had only his own strength to hang on to in these darkest hours.

When the Baroness opened her eyes, he was there holding her hand. She looked up at him dazedly.

Weakly, she asked, 'What happened?'

'You fainted, madame.' Ravel was there smiling down on her reassuringly. 'Collapse through strain. It happens to us all if we do not take care. You must rest for at least three days in bed. I insist. Then you must take it easy for a while.'

She regarded him with a kind of horror before looking appealingly at her son.

'I cannot! You know I have to go to Paris with your father, Armand,' she said in desperation.

Armand leaned forward to speak gently as though to a child. 'I shall be with Papa, so why not stay here with Sara who will look after you? I can phone you everyday to keep you in touch with what goes on.'

'But if he asks for me?.

'Then I shall come for you at once.'

Colour came back slowly to her ashen face. Her lips trembled into a smile and a long shuddering sigh came from the deep recesses of her heart.

'As you say, Armand. I will stay with Sara. What would I do without you both?'

Sara was deeply moved. For the Comtesse to acknowledge her son's wife and couple her with him even in the midst of her distress was something she would never forget. Later, when Armand had gone with his father and Monsieur Ravel to Paris, she was left with the memory of a thin gaunt face and closed sunken eyes as the Comte, swathed in blankets, was carried to the ambulance.

The Comtesse slept most of that day under a sedative from the doctor. Armand had phoned him before he left for Paris and his verdict when he had arrived was much the same as Monsieur Ravel's. A few days' rest in bed, then to take things easy for a while.

It was ten o'clock that evening when Sara went into her mother-in-law's room to have a nightcap with her. She entered the lovely room with its pastel-coloured decor, enchanting in the flickering firelight, to find her awake and sitting up in bed. The soft turquoise bedjacket she wore gave her a youthful air and she looked rested.

Sara walked to the bed. 'Well, how do you feel?' she asked gently, warmly.

'Much better, I think. Céline has left a tray.' She looked at Sara appraisingly. 'How delicious and sweet you look,' as she received her kiss. 'And you smell divine. What is it?'

'English cologne,' answered Sara matter-of-factly. She was wearing a negligée of frothy white laced with blue ribbon. Fresh from her recent bath, her face was free from make-up and her pale silky hair was tied back with blue ribbon.

The Comtesse watched the small slender hands manipulating the silver jug as Sara filled two glasses with hot milk. What a delightful person she was, she thought, fresh and sweet like an English rose. Her graceful movements and gentle concentration on the task in hand enchanted her. No wonder Armand loved her so much!

The Comtesse had often conjectured on the kind of woman her son would marry, hoping naturally that he would choose a Frenchwoman. Her disappointment on hearing his bride was English was soon forgotten when she met Sara. She had taken to her on sight, finding some kind of inner contact, some strange powerful bond drawing them together instantly. There had been moments when she had seen a look of infinite sadness on her daughter-in-law's face when she thought she was unobserved which puzzled her. The Comtesse would have welcomed her confidence, but had wisely decided to wait until it was offered. Had her husband not been so seriously ill, she would have thought the same about Armand too. He certainly had not been his usual self since his marriage. His unhappiness, of course, was over his father. They were a closely knit family. The last thing she wanted was to interfere. Sensibly, she was of the opinion that young people, unless they asked for advice, were best left to sort out their own problems. This reason, and the fact that Sara was as yet an unknown quantity here she was concerned, kept her silent.

She accepted her glass of hot milk and watched Sara curl up in a chair by the bed with her bare feet tucked under her.

'You look about twelve,' the Comtesse told her mischievously, thinking how like gems were the deep blue eyes regarding her soberly. 'I am going to love your children, Sara. Armand adores children and they always adore him.'

The Poulain charm, mused Sara wryly, to which even babes in arms were not immune. Rather disconcerted, she attempted to make a light rejoinder.

'To tell you the truth, I hadn't given it a thought. It's something to know your husband likes children. Some men don't.'

Her hands curled nervously round her glass. Not until that moment did she realize how wrong she had been to enter into holy matrimony on a wave of vengeance. It was a violation of a sacred union between two people. Sara could imagine the look of horror on the face of the Comtesse when she discovered what a farce her son's marriage really was. Too bad she was such a nice person, so nice that Sara was again sorely tempted to confide in her and tell her the truth. But it would take a harder heart than hers to blacken Armand still further in his mother's eyes. Her quarrel was not with the Comtesse and she shrank from hurting her any more than was necessary.

'Do you like children, Sara?'

Startled out of unhappy thoughts, Sara met the kindly gaze. Disconcerted by the unexpected question, her face burned hotly. 'Yes, I adore them ... only our marriage happened so quickly, I still seem to be finding my bearings,' she replied warily. 'I'm sure they're essential for a happy marriage.'

She knew she was talking rather woodenly. But for the life of her, she could not infuse any kind of feeling into her words. How she hated the deceit, hated Armand too for thrusting her still further into acting it. Was it her fancy, or did the Comtesse look at her rather guardedly for a fleeting second?

'I am of the same opinion,' she was saying. 'I know Armand would be very disappointed not to have them.'

This alerted Sara like a prod in the ribs. Naturally he would want an heir. The thought made her go hot all over. He was just the kind of man to demand one. She felt distinctly odd and more than frightened.

'Has he said so?'

'No, no. One senses these things. Armand keeps his own counsel. We have brought him up to be self-sufficient – to work out his own problems. Perhaps to you, knowing him so little, he appears to be arrogant and demanding. He is essentially a man first and a lover second. Like his father, he is apt to spoil his womenfolk.' She smiled, the smile of a proud mother with all her love for her son in her eyes. 'You will find him a devoted husband. You will never have anything to worry about. I am deeply sorry that the Comte's illness is keeping you apart at a time when you should be discovering each other. However,' the shadow in her eyes was fleeting, 'you must take a prolonged honeymoon when my husband is better, which I pray will be very soon.'

It couldn't be too soon for me, Sara thought. 'I pray that he will soon recover too,' she said sincerely. 'As for being on our honeymoon, Armand explained that he had to stay within call of his office in Paris for a short while, so we haven't really started a honeymoon yet. You have nothing to reproach yourself with on that score. No one can help illness, and what is a family for if not to stand together in moments of crisis?'

'How sweet of you to be so sensible about it. Most young women would resent being parted from their husband so soon, and Armand is spending time with his father he would normally have spent with you. We cannot even give a party for you to meet all our friends, and I assure you they are all dying to meet you, until my poor husband is better. I am very grateful to you for being such a sport about it, Sara, and I love you for it.'

Sara flinched inwardly. If only she knew! Her hand trembled as she put down her empty glass. 'I would say it works both ways. I am more than grateful to you for welcoming me into your home and accepting me whole-heartedly as your son's wife without prejudice.'

The sudden shrill ringing of the phone beside the bed startled them both and the Comtesse put down her empty glass to pick up the receiver.

'Armand? Yes, I am much better. How is your father. Has he asked for me? Oh!' – an audible sigh. 'I am happy to know he stood the journey so well. Yes, I understand it will take time for tests to be made. And Monsieur Ravel is satisfied with him? Yes, Sara is here with me now, looking after me like a daughter. I wish you could see her. She looks delicious in her white negligé laced with blue – but I suppose you have seen her in it. I am sorry for your honeymoon to be spoilt like this. Are you feeling very bitter against it? Bearing up like Sara, bless her. Thank you for her, Armand. I already love her like a daughter. Your father will love her too.'

An unwilling listener, Sara could imagine Armand's mouth curling with a sardonic twist at the other end of the phone. Was he remembering their leavetaking when he had left for Paris with his father and Monsieur Ravel? She had perforce gone out with him to see him off, and he had acted like the loving bridegroom. Sara had been unable to define the expression in his face as he had taken her into his arms – critical, searching, mocking – or cruel. It could have been any of them. But there was no mistaking the bitter humour about his mouth as he bent his head. His kiss had been hard and cruel, bruising her lips and leaving her shakenly bereft of her senses. With the taste of blood on her lips, Sara had hardened her heart, realizing it was the real Armand, cruel and absolutely without feeling as he had been with Maura. When the Comtesse handed her the phone to have a word with him, she was perfectly controlled.

'How is Maman?' was his first question. 'She assures me she is much better, but I want your opinion.'

'She looks much better.' She waited, thinking he had rung off, then he spoke again.

'Sara.' The deep voice lingered over her name and she trembled in spite of her armour. 'Thank you for keeping my mother happy.'

The concern in his tone aroused strange emotions, not jealousy, for she knew how shallow his feelings were. Yet she was disturbed nevertheless. Even so her voice was well modulated with the right degree of sweetness.

'I'm so happy to know your father is all right after his journey.'

'*Merci.*' His voice was suddenly void of expression. 'It is too early to say, but I am living in hopes of his complete recovery and none the worse for his illness. I shall return as soon as something definite is known. I suppose you cannot wait for me to give you your release?'

The last words were loaded with sarcasm, and Sara, aware of his mother's presence in the room, bit back a suitable retort. Instead, she cooed in the manner of a pining bride, 'Darling, you don't know how much I long for your return.'

Dead silence at the other end of the phone, then, 'I take it Maman is in the room with you?'

'Darling, of course.' Sara would have loved to have seen his face.

'Of course,' he echoed. 'You will let me know if she is ill again and insist that she rests?'

'I will. I adore her.'

'But not me.' He waited for her to answer and when none was forthcoming, he bade her *bonne nuit.*

'*Bonne nuit*, darling,' she whispered for his mother's benefit, waiting with suspended breath for his reaction to the endearment. But there was nothing, only the decisive click of the phone as he laid it down.

Sara put down the receiver, hoping her act had passed muster with his mother. She had kept her head turned away from the bed in order to hide the expressions on her face brought into play by the farce she had to act to the bitter end. Had his mother not been present the necessity to keep up appearances would not have arisen. The Comtesse was lying back on her pillow with her eyes closed.

Sara left her chair. 'Are you all right, dear?' she asked, bending over her anxiously.

The hazel eyes were brimming over with tears. 'Just a little overwhelmed with relief to know there is hope of my beloved getting better. I could not conceive of life without him.' Her trembling lips made further words impossible for the moment and she blinked hastily. 'Please forgive me for behaving like this. As if you had not enough to contend with – a bride all alone on her honeymoon!'

Sara straightened the bed clothes, taking the older woman's arms gently and covering them up. 'I think you are being very brave about it,' she said warmly. 'Now will you stop tormenting yourself about me and concentrate upon getting well. The sooner you are well, the sooner you can go to see your husband. Now go to sleep. I shall sit beside you until you do.'

Sara kissed the Comtesse on her forehead and sat down beside her. Sitting silent in the shadow, Sara realized with a sense of shock how insidiously the bonds of affection were clinging and growing with the strength of creepers around her heart. Listening to the even breathing of the Comtesse, now sleeping peacefully, she contemplated upon the disillusionment awaiting her mother-in-law when she found out the truth. How she would despise her, not only for deceiving her but for the hurt to her son. Sara could not bear to think about it. Yet it had to be faced.

# CHAPTER NINE

SARA left her bed the following morning as soon as it was light, put on her riding clothes and after peeping in on the Comtesse to make sure she was still asleep, went down to the stables. Mimi was a joy to ride, cavorting gently and whinneying with delight when Sara gave her her head.

Flags of colour tinted Sara's face as they sped along paths dappled with early morning sunshine on the fringe of woods slowly coming to life with the soft rustle of trees shaking off the effects of sleep. In the midst of her enjoyment, she spared a thought for Armand's father and hoped with all her heart that his recovery would be swift and successful. She could have stayed out all the glorious morning, but the thought of the Comtesse limited her ride to an hour. Even then she returned to the stables feeling a little guilty.

After a wash and change, she went to her mother-in-law's room to find her sitting up in bed. Céline had washed and dressed her in a white bedjacket trimmed with swansdown and combed her hair neatly.

'Bonjour, Sara,' she said, putting out her hands in greeting. 'How fresh and glowing you look!'

Sara bent to kiss the perfumed cheek. 'You are looking better too. Have you had a good night?'

'Lovely. I slept until half an hour ago and I am ready for breakfast. Céline is bringing it on a tray.' She held on to Sara's hand, clasping it warmly. 'You have not had breakfast? Céline said you had not been down to the dining-room.'

'No, I haven't. I've been for a ride on Mimi and I've thoroughly enjoyed it.'

'Bien. Then you can have breakfast with me.' The Comtesse released Sara's hand as Céline entered with a tray.

Over freshly buttered croissants, they talked – or at least the Comtesse did. With the hope of her husband's possible recovery uppermost in her mind she had plenty to tell her daughter-in-law about friends of the family and neighbours whom Sara would meet. There would be parties to give and parties to attend, but all this, of course, when Sara and Armand returned from their honeymoon.

And Sara had to listen knowing she was going to miss a wonderful friendship with a woman who had made her feel as wanted as her own mother might have done. In the warm friendliness of the Comtesse's charm, Sara talked and laughed and was, for the time being, happy.

The next two days brought a peace she had not known for a long time. Sara spent most of her time with the Comtesse in her room, talking, reading and making herself generally useful and saving Céline small jobs made extra through her mistress being indisposed. Friends of the family called or phoned, but none were admitted on the doctor's orders. He came each day, but insisted on his patient staying in bed for at least two days.

Armand phoned each evening at ten with news of his father, who was still undergoing tests. Armand's attitude to Sara was coldly polite at his end of the phone, whereas Sara had to play out the farce of the deserted bride waiting to welcome her husband back with open arms. It had been extremely difficult to infuse the right amount of fervour into the short conversation she had with him in the presence of his mother. But she managed it, bolstered by the fact that when his father was on the road to recovery, she could leave.

On the third day the doctor allowed the Comtesse to get up after breakfast. She looked much better after her rest in bed, when, with her tailored cream skirt smooth over neat hips and a narrow belt holding her cream silk shirt in place, she had coffee with Sara in the lounge.

'It is far too nice to stay indoors, Sara,' she mused, looking out from the tall windows to pools of sunlight on the lawns and flower beds. 'What do you say to going across to the Petit Chateau? Since Armand is not here to show you around, today is as good as any to see it. Besides, it will be at its best in the sun.'

'Are you sure you feel up to it?' Sara asked, hiding her dismay at the prospect of looking through an establishment which would never be part of her life. It surprised her to discover that she would hate to remember it later and think of Armand taking his wife there. There would be babies too. But the Comtesse looked so pleased at the thought that Sara had not the heart to refuse. There was a kind of fatality about it – as if she had to run through the whole gamut of emotions to the bitter end of the final denouncement.

So, mute and unresisting, she walked with the Comtesse through the grounds of the estate beneath huge old trees shedding their spring blossom like perfumed confetti at their feet. She had decided to be unimpressed by the Petit Chateau. But the moment she saw it, Sara fell in love with it.

The Petit Chateau was a mini-chateau with all the dignity of a Chatsworth House set in a nest of Lombardy poplars. Sara was enchanted.

'Perfect!' Her voice was little more than a whisper. 'Can we go inside now?'

The Comtesse was pleased. 'Certainly. One day each week fires are lighted in all the rooms to air them, and the front door will be open.'

'So it is.'

Sara looked towards the entrance door and the arch above it displaying the family crest. A fire burned in the fireplace in the hall, sending out a fragrance of apple logs. Every room was fragrant with them and Sara found it incredible for a place to remain so fresh after being unoccupied for years. Furniture and furnishings gleamed richly with a cherished well-preserved look from devoted hands.

The nursery where Armand had crawled from babyhood to boyhood still contained his childhood treasures. Sharply, Sara turned her head away from a big rocking horse in a corner of the room. Armand's presence was so real in that disturbing second that Sara fully expected him to come striding into the room. Shutting him from her thoughts did not dismiss the fact that it would be heaven to live in this enchanting place where the only shadows were warmed by the dim beauty in the rooms.

Sara listened as her mother-in-law told of the time she came to the Chateau as a very happy bride. 'I do want you to be as happy here as I have been, Sara.' They had returned to the hall after a tour of the house. 'You fit in so well. I have no doubt you will be.' She gave a small laugh as though shedding a private worry. 'To think I was a little apprehensive when I heard Armand had married an Englishwoman! But I must confess I was very relieved when I met you. I only hope you will not become bored with country life.'

'Why should I, when it has so much to offer? I love the walks, the riding, swimming and skiing.' In that moment Sara only remembered the happy times spent with Armand on the skiing slopes. 'Did Armand tell you he took me skiing?'

'No. He has won endless cups for it and is an excellent sportsman like his father.'

The Comtesse turned her face away, overcome with emotion on mentioning her husband. But it had been a mother speaking – a mother full of pride in her son. Sara knew then with a sinking heart that when the time came for her to go the Comtesse must know nothing about her marriage for revenge. She must never know how callously Armand had treated Maura unless he chose to tell her himself. She must be allowed to keep her illusions. Sara's excuse for the break-up of her marriage would be that the boredom of life in the country had proved too much for her, after all, and she was going back to London.

She was dressing for dinner that evening when she heard the car on the drive pull up with a shrieking of brakes as though the driver had been travelling with his foot pressed down on the accelerator. Armand. Sara never heard the shrieking of car brakes afterwards without thinking of him. His unexpected arrival, his exuberant force and overflowing energy made manifest by a disciplined grace brought an air of excitement to the tranquillity of the Chateau.

Sara, in a state of undress, rushed from the window to

seize the first evening gown her shaking fingers came into contact with. Stepping into the foam of sea blue chiffon billowing around her feet, she reached behind her for the zip. It came up beautifully to her waist, then stuck, defying all her efforts to move it.

She was still struggling with it when the peremptory tap came on her door. It would be Céline. Sara bade her enter, never doubting for a moment that Armand would go straight to his mother before coming to his room.

'Hello, Sara.'

Armand closed the door and leaned back against it. A slow sense of shock propelled her round to face him, unaware of her bare back being reflected in the dressing table mirror behind her. All her preparation, the armour she had built up around her for his coming, disintegrated beneath that intent dark gaze. A chill feathered across her skin although her face burned.

'This . . . is a surprise,' she croaked nervously. 'How is your father? Not worse, I hope?'

'As well as can be expected,' he replied laconically, one dark eyebrow elevated at her reflection in the mirror. 'Having trouble?'

Sara stared at him blankly in an effort to gather her scattered wits. 'Oh, the zip? I'm expecting Céline at any moment.'

He crossed the room in a couple of strides and was manipulating the zip before she could stop him. For breathless palpitating moments he bent over the slender lines of her lovely back before drawing the zip up gently to cover it. The sudden contact with the cold zip against her skin made Sara shudder. She felt him hesitate after using the hook at the top of the zip when his fingers had touched her neck as he fastened it. Then he had dropped his hands immediately.

'Thanks,' she said, turning round once more to face him, to see his face set pale beneath his tan. His eyes were blacker than ever, his jaw rigid. He was like a man dealt a mortal blow. It would not occur to him that the cold zip was responsible for her shudder and that it was not a shudder of revulsion when his fingers had touched her neck. Sara's sensitivity urged her to enlighten him. Then she hardened her heart. Why should she? He had hurt Maura without a qualm. If he was hurt then it was another blow given on her behalf. 'Have you seen your mother?' She spoke quickly – anything to take the iron mask from his face.

It was the old insolent, arrogant Armand who answered. 'I have, and believe it or not, I was sent along to my pining bride who shivers with revulsion at my touch.'

Colour came up in a dark tide over her face and neck. 'I'm sorry . . .'

'Please, no apology for hating me. You must have been pretty convincing while I was away, for Maman regards us as a couple of lovebirds. Had I not had other things on my mind I would not have forgotten how good you are at putting on an act. Too bad that instead of being a happy bride you are a poor child at the mercy of a bad, bad man who lures young women to their deaths.' His eyes hardening took in her fairness. 'That is how you regard me, is it not?'

It seemed to Sara that all the arrogance had left his dark set features and a look like that of a boy unjustly accused had taken its place, making her feel weak and weepy. Then it was gone, replaced by a look of contempt, and she braced herself for what she must do. There was no going back along the road she had taken. She had to do what she felt was right and gather enough strength to do it.

'I know what you did to my best friend,' she uttered between pale lips. 'I'm never likely to forget it.' She clenched her hands as the whole thing became too much to be borne. The farce had to be ended here and now. 'There's no sense in my staying here for us to throw brickbats at each other. I should never have allowed you to persuade me to stay in the first place, although I'm happy to have been able to help your mother.' The words tumbled from her lips in all their bitterness. She was unable to stop their flow. 'I shall pack tonight and you must do as you wish about an annulment. I shall leave a letter for your mother telling her that life in the country is too dead for one who's used to city life. You can tell her what you choose, but don't hurt her more than is necessary.' To her dismay tears gathered in her eyes. 'Too bad you didn't inherit some of her fine qualities. My lawyers will get in touch with you.'

She thought, Thank heaven this is the end. A numbness around her heart spread slowly over her body and she stood very still, trying to compel herself to calmness.

If she could have walked away, she would have done. But there was nowhere to walk to. Armand looked down at her keenly with those disconcerting black eyes, his dark intent face enigmatically controlled. Then, straightening, he walked to the fireplace to place his arm along the top of the high mantelpiece and gaze down into the fire.

'You must do as you wish,' he began. 'But before you do so I feel I should tell you what I have not told anyone else, not even Maman. My father is dangerously ill. Ravel says it is essential for him to act swiftly. He has asked my permission to use a new drug which will give my father a fifty-fifty chance of recovering.' He drew a rasping breath. 'It is a decision I have to take alone. In view of Maman's recent collapse, Ravel advised me not to tell her. In any case I could not subject her to the agony it involves – twenty-four hours of hell while we wait for the result, plus the fact that if it fails my father's death will lie at my door.'

'I'm sorry.' Sara looked down at her hands clasped demurely in front of her. 'What you have told me can in no way alter my decision to leave as soon as possible. I feel it would be wrong if I stayed and allowed your mother to become dependent on my company. Better to go now before our parting causes her more pain. She has friends who will rally round if needed.'

He said forcibly, 'You are more than a friend. You are family, someone close in whom she can confide.'

'I'm well aware of that,' Sara answered more firmly. 'I'm also determined to put an end to this farce of being something I'm not.'

'You will eventually. I have no more desire than you to cling to a loveless marriage.'

Sara drew in a shuddering breath, drenched by the wave of desolation sweeping over her. Her thoughts whirled, round not making sense. She was a fool to hesitate.

He continued on a jeering note which jarred, 'What has happened to that burning desire for revenge? Cold feet? I am disappointed in you. I thought you had more spirit. Surely by giving up now you are missing the most enjoyable part of your victory? Think how you will enjoy watching my grief if my father dies.'

The words hurt and blistered. Sara recoiled, clenching the palms of her hands until the nails dug in painfully. Her colour rose, then faded to a waxen pallor. She was overwhelmed by an agony of remembered misery and pain. How dared he?

'Stop it!' she cried. Her head suddenly thrown back, Sara met his black-browed look with blazing blue eyes. 'You're making me out as some kind of vampire out to suck your blood. What I've done is in keeping with how I felt about Maura – how I still feel. She couldn't hit back at you. I could.'

'And you did.' He straightened, his black ironic gaze intent upon her with an expression she could not fathom. 'You succeeded beyond your wildest dreams, *ma petite*. Your little arrow of vengeance scored a direct hit through the heart. I loved you as a man loves only once in a lifetime. I have never loved any woman as I loved you.' He paused for his words to take effect, then added with a cold deliberation, 'At least I loved the woman I thought you were, not this hard-eyed, hard-hearted female you turned out to be.' Suddenly his mood changed. He was again the old arrogant Armand with the deadly charm whose smile lighted up the room but not his eyes. 'Suppose we forget this feud between us? The score is settled. Shall we go on from here?'

Sara stiffened. 'What do you mean?' she asked warily.

'Another day or so is not going to make much difference to you either way. I will put it like this. I am the villain of the piece who is keeping you here against your will. You are the fair maiden imprisoned in the Chateau who has to look after my mother until it is convenient for the villain to release you.'

He raised black brows and Sara murmured her thoughts aloud. 'The King of Spades.'

'*Touché* – the wicked King of Spades it is,' he agreed, in no whit dismayed. 'Yet I have a sweet mother. Amazing, is it not?' Thrusting his hands into his pockets, he strolled nonchalantly to the window where he went on speaking with his back towards her. 'I would be grateful if you would agree to stay for the next few days. It might not be very pleasant for you, for if my father should die I would ask you to remain until after the funeral.' His voice had thickened and he had to clear his throat before he could go on. 'Afterwards, I would take Maman abroad for a while. If you feel you cannot face it, I shall understand. But I think you like Maman enough to do as I ask.'

Sara had an appalling sense of being caught in a trap of her own making. He had loved her, he said, using the past tense, which meant he did not love her now. He was probably hating her as much as she was hating him. The thought brought the dew to her temples. She knew he was going through purgatory, for there was no anticipatory look in the dark eyes that met her own, no hope even of her acquiescence.

In the face of so much agony, Sara had to be kind. Besides, she was very fond of his mother. 'Very well.' She met his tormented gaze with a brief smile. 'I will stay as long as it's necessary.' The dryness of her throat lent a huskiness to her voice. 'I sincerely hope your father recovers, and soon.' Unconsciously, she put out a hand and he clasped it firmly. His eyes held a sad disenchantment, but they were still alluring enough to bring the blood to her face.

'I am more than grateful.' He spoke without expression. 'Ravel is waiting for my answer. Would to God I knew the right one!'

'You do,' Sara assured him, allowing her hand to remain in his. 'If your father could choose he would take the sporting chance no matter what the odds.'

His clasp on her hand tightened. 'You think that?'

Sara nodded. 'I'm sure of it. I'm going by his son. Whatever you are, whatever you've been, you too would take that chance.'

Armand looked down at her for a long moment, his tired eyes finding a wisdom and a strength in her equal to his own. 'Bless you, *mon amie*,' he murmured, and kissed her hand.

Tears welled from deep inside her. He had called her his friend, not his darling. The words were a sword thrust to her heart. She had destroyed her own image in his eyes. Why should she care? But she knew she did enormously.

Sara's truce with Armand lightened the atmosphere at dinner that evening considerably. With his mother seated at the head of the table, Sara sat opposite Armand to dine *en famille* in the charming dining room. The table was gay with crystal glass and silver and spring flowers beautifully arranged between tall red candles.

Armand talked easily and charmingly to his mother and Sara. He had convinced the Comtesse that his fleeting visit home was to see his two loves, Sara and herself. Consequently his mother had accepted it with a twinkle in her eye and a 'Bless you, my children,' look. She was, however, determined to go to Paris when the doctor gave her permission to travel. Once there, she was planning to stay with her husband until he was well enough to come home.

Sara sat in uneasy silence listening to her mother-in-law making plans, confident in her husband's recovery, in the hands of Monsieur Ravel. During the meal Sara had left the conversation to Armand and his mother. There was no bored insolence about him now, and although his every movement suggested latent strength he looked tired, his eyes so dark that Sara wanted to lose herself in their blackness. But there was none of those burning glances which had so often held her blue eyes against their will. Sara was annoyed to find herself wanting those thrilling glances which had played havoc with her heart. But on the few occasions she had found him looking at her covertly, there had been an instantaneous hardening of his dark eyes and he had looked away with a set expression of neutrality.

After dinner they all sat by the log fire listening to records. Armand sat with one arm along the back of the sofa companionably near to Sara's slim shoulders as she sat beside him. The Comtesse sat in a gold-fringed winged chair on the opposite side of the fireplace. It was like her thoughtfulness to retire early in order to give Armand and Sara some time on their own.

Sara had watched her leave in dismay, as she had nothing to say to Armand. Perhaps he was just as uncomfortable, for when the last long-playing record ended, he suggested taking a short walk in the grounds before retiring. He allowed her to precede him into the hall, then left her while he took the stairs two at a time to fetch her evening wrap from her room. He really was the most amazing man, she thought, wishing she knew the real one among the many roles he played.

He came downstairs in a matter of minutes with her white woollen jacket which he draped around her shoulders and she thanked him with a cool little smile. But Sara was far from cool inside. Much as she tried to, she found it impossible to ignore the wide expanse of shoulder, erect and arrogant, his arm swinging near to her side with the brown, long-fingered hand jutting from the white silk cuff and his dark, sardonic profile, blackbrowed and brooding.

The moon cast mysterious shadows as they walked towards the stables. All was quiet, for the horses had retired for the night, but the rustle of freshly strewn straw in one of the boxes caused Armand to pause and open the top half of the door carefully. The brown head appeared immediately to give a soft whinney of pleasure. With a laugh, Armand was at once boyish and carefree as he fondled the soft nose and gave the mare two sugar lumps from his pocket.

'*Doucement*,' he whispered softly when the mare gave him a gentle push with her head. To Sara, he said, 'My favourite mare, Mistral. I had her when I was a boy. She is my most precious possession. Are you not, *ma chère*?'

Sara lifted a hand to stroke the long satiny neck, sure she could see a twinkle in the soft brown eyes. The next moment the mare had playfully pushed her against Armand and instantly his arm was around her waist to steady her.

'You're as light as thistledown,' he looked down at her mockingly. 'No wonder she knocked you off balance. Did she hurt you?'

'No,' she whispered. 'She's delicious.'

Something urgent and compelling in his voice touched her strangely. Feeling rather odd, she moved out of the circle of his arm, aware of being on dangerous ground to pat Mistral's head. I've willed myself to hate him, she mused, and how difficult it is at times. He's so very male, so devilishly attractive, this King of Spades whom Maura loved in vain. Maura. Pain stabbed as memories tormented her.

She was very quiet during that short walk through the grounds and they were retracing their steps back to the Chateau when he said, 'So Maman has taken you around the Petit Chateau? What do you think about it?'

'I was enchanted.'

'*Bien*,' he commented, and was silent.

Glancing at his enigmatic profile, Sara felt they could not be further apart had oceans divided them. He bade her good night at the foot of the stairs.

'Sara.'

Her name on his lips as she reached the fourth step reverberated along her nerves. She turned, outwardly serene, her cheeks brilliant with colour, her hair a pale misty sheen above the brilliance of her eyes giving her an ethereal look, a vulnerable one. He looked up at her with the alluring spark deep down in his black eyes surfacing slowly. And Sara, looking below the surface, saw the hidden agony and knew a great compassion as he said heavily as if against his will, 'I have decided to give Ravel a free hand.'

# CHAPTER TEN

Sara awoke after a night of tormenting dreams to see two
letters on her bedside table. Her face grew hot on recognizing Armand's masculine scrawl on the top one. He must
have come into her room to leave them. There was no
sound coming from the adjoining room, so he had already
left, presumably for Paris. The dull ache in her head
brought on through a restless night increased with a
vague premoniton when, on picking up the second letter,
she saw it was from Major Penhurst. What was Maura's
father writing to her about? She opened Armand's letter
first.

'I shall be back later today,' he had written. 'I thought
it best to tell Maman that Ravel was putting Papa on a
new drug and that he had to be left alone for twenty-four
hours after it was administrated. She has no idea of the
gravity of the situation, but I have promised to take her
to him afterwards. It will either be one thing or the other.
Pray God it will be the cure we are seeking. Armand.'

A wave of depression swept over Sara as she put the
letter down. The morning was not too bright. The
window framed a grey patch of sky slashed with angry
red menacing streaks, the air was humid. Sara shivered
and thought of Armand returning home to go through
twenty-four hours of agonizing dread. It would be fatal to
allow compassion to override common sense, she
reasoned. I know Armand treated Maura badly and when
I leave here I mustn't think about him again. It would
not be easy to forget him. Those days of intimate companionship on the skiing slopes had been carefree – or
almost. I shall never be carefree again, she thought, with
an intolerable ache in her heart.

Wearily, she opened Major Penhurst's letter.

My dear Sara, it began. I am more sorry than I can say
to be the bearer of bad news, but here it is. My dear wife
passed away and was buried yesterday alongside Maura

in the village churchyard. I humbly apologize for not letting you know sooner, but I thought it best not to call you home from a holiday you so badly needed. I have written to Julian and I hope he too will forgive me for not letting him know soon enough for him to come over for the funeral. It was all so sudden and I am still too shocked to take it in. As you know, my wife has not been the same woman since we lost our beloved daughter. She died in her sleep from natural causes, having lost the will to live. My only consolation is to know that she is with Maura and therefore at peace. I look forward to seeing you when you return. We must have a chat about the horses you left in my care, for I am selling up and clearing out to join my brother in Canada. Do not grieve too much, and look after yourself, Yours with deep affection, Ronald Penhurst.

Beyond tears and deeply shocked, Sara found it impossible to think calmly about it. Scenes from the past rose unbidden before her eyes – Maura playing tennis on the courts at Penhurst Towers, riding in the horse trials, taking home her trophies, laughing her way through hunt balls and birthday parties. Then the tragedy. Masses of floral tributes when her body was brought home, the whispers of horror and sympathy, Jean Penhurst's face suddenly old beyond her years – a stricken mother robbed of the light of her life. And all because of one man – Armand Romond de Poulain. Sara's hand clenched on the letter. Curse him!

Half demented, she left her bed with an urge to get away from the four walls which seemed to be closing in on her. Had she been able to think rationally, she would have packed her cases and gone. But all she could think about was fresh air and some wide open space where she could think. Only half aware of what she was doing, she put on her riding things and went swiftly downstairs. The crimson gashes of light in the grey sky sent a rosy glow through the soft morning mist as Sara approached the stables, to see Jean-Paul walking away from a horse he had already saddled – Mistral. Sara was in no mood to see Jean-Paul or anyone, and suddenly she had swung herself up on to Mistral's back.

Heavy drops of rain pelted down as she gave Mistral her head to gallop across country. The mare pricked her ears once or twice and whinneyed at the sound of distant thunder. But Sara urged her on alongside the turbulent waters of the river as grey as the sheets of rain, lashing it to fury. Tears were now rolling unchecked down her face to mingle with the rain. In the agony of her grief, she was hardly aware of the damp chilliness to her body as gradually her clothes became soaked with the rain. Her heart was torn apart by the thought of yet another beloved figure being taken from her little circle spelling security.

A horrible fear mingled with her grief – a fear of never knowing any real security – of always being on her own with no one belonging. She had come up against that same fear when her father died. But Julian had stepped into the breach then, and there were the Penhursts. Now Julian had gone, and soon the last of her dear friends the Penhursts would be gone too. As for marrying herself some day, Armand had spoiled her for that. How could one trust a man, any man, when they could be fascinating and charming and a villain to boot?

Sobs rose from deep inside her as she faced the blinding rain. Branches of trees creaked beneath the deluge and the steady pattering on shapes looming suddenly out of the mist took on an ominous sound. The first shaft of lightning pierced the sky viciously, lighting everywhere with a frightening glow. Mistral whinneyed and blew steam through her nostrils as the thunder rolled. She was going on at a pace now along a path now fast becoming waterlogged.

Mistral was straining to keep her balance along the treacherously slippery path and Sara surfaced from her own heavy breathing and the thunder of hooves to realize that she was pushing the mare beyond her endurance. Alerted at last to the danger, she turned Mistral round and made for the Chateau. Several times the mare slipped then miraculously gained her balance. They were in sight of the Chateau when Mistral fell heavily and Sara, rolling clear, hit her head sharply against the roots of a tree.

When she came round the rain had stopped and the sun was shining fitfully between scudding black clouds. Feeling giddy, she sat up on the wet ground feeling her limbs for any damage and calling herself all kinds of a fool for coming out in such weather – on Mistral too. Armand would be furious. Well, let him! What did she care? Pushing back the wet hair from her forehead, Sara rose painfully to her feet. No limbs appeared to be broken, but the fall had shaken her severely and her head throbbed agonizingly. The sweet smell of wet earth filled her nostrils and all around her raindrops glistened diamond-bright on the foliage of trees – and then she saw Mistral.

Feeling suddenly icy cold in her wet clothes and with her boots quelching at every step, Sara approached the mare. Mistral lay on her side ominously still. The next moment Sara recoiled in horror. Mistral was dead. She fell across the wet body, her face crumpled against the mare's neck and sobbed her heart out. How long she lay there she never knew, having lost all count of time in her grief.

At last, she stumbled to her feet and made her way back mechanically to the chateau. Jean-Paul was in the stable yard staring at her dishevelled appearance.

'Has there been an accident, madame?' he asked politely, eyeing her saturated look and muddy clothes in concern. 'I saw you go on Mistral, but I knew she would be all right with you.' But words were beyond Sara and he went on, 'I had saddled her for a short ride before the rain began. It is my custom when Monsieur is away to exercise the horses.'

Sara's lips trembled. She closed her eyes as fresh tears squeezed through in between wet lashes. 'There has been an accident,' she said, hating herself and everyone except poor Mistral. 'Mistral fell on the way back . . . Oh, Jean-Paul, Mistral is dead!'

She fled then – fled from Jean-Paul's shocked face and wishing she had died there with Mistral. Her eyes blurred with tears and half hysterical, she failed to see the car at the entrance door of the Chateau and it was not until Armand stopped her headlong flight by gripping her arms firmly that she realized he was there.

His concern at her appearance lent an edge to his voice. 'Why, you are soaked! What happened?' He looked startled. 'You surely have not been out riding in that storm?'

She struggled violently out of his arms. 'Let me go! I hate you! You ... you devil incarnate!' she cried vehemently.

He barred her way frowning heavily and took hold of her arms again, ignoring her struggles. 'I demand to know what has happened. Were you thrown? Are you hurt?'

'What do you care? If you want to know, I've been out on Mistral.'

His look was puzzled. His face set and the black eyes smouldered. 'You must be mad to go out riding on a morning like this!'

'Not now. I have been made to stay here, but I'm sane enough now, sane enough to know what a fool I've been in listening to you, in allowing you to persuade me to stay here against my will.' Sara pushed a weary hand childishly across her eyes. They were swollen with weeping and she gave a long shuddering sigh while tears and hysterical laughter warred in her throat. 'I don't think even you will stop me from leaving when you know Mistral is dead.'

A strange whiteness crept up from his neck beneath the bronze skin. His grip made her wince. 'Dead?' he repeated, glowering down at her. 'What do you mean?

'What I say.' Sara controlled the trembling of her lips with an effort. 'Mistral is dead.'

He stood for several minutes probing her face mercilessly. Then his eyes blazed and just as she thought he was going to do something terrible in his anger, he drew in a rasping breath. 'Why, you little . . .' He stopped short at calling her some name which she felt was horrible to look broodingly into her face. 'So you used poor Mistral to further your revenge upon me. How you must hate me! You knew how much I loved her and you took her out deliberately to her death.'

It was Sara's turn to stare up unbelievingly into his dark face. It had never occurred to her that her impulsive action in taking Mistral out would be misconstrued. Her lips felt as white as her face. 'You . . . you actually think I took Mistral out to hurt her?'

'Why else but to hurt me in the end?'

All her anger suddenly fled. How could she tell him about Jean Penhurst, about anything? She spoke slowly with a kind of dull despair. 'I think you're the most despicable man I've ever met!'

She ran around him, through the entrance door of the Chateau, across the hall and up the stairs to her room, where she tore off her sodden clothes and went under the shower. A knock came on her door as she reached for a towel. Her first reaction was to ignore it. Hastily she dried her wet limbs and thrust her arms into a wrap. When the knock was repeated gently, Sara thought of the Comtesse and regardless of her dripping hair, went to open the door. But it was not the Comtesse, it was Céline.

'Monsieur sent this warm drink, madame. I believe you have had an accident and I am sorry.' She was in the room and putting down the tray to look at Sara's working face before Sara could collect herself. 'Do sit down while I dry your hair. You look exhausted.'

Sara sank down into the nearest chair and allowed Céline to dry her hair with a towel fetched hastily from the bathroom. The vigorous rubbing of her scalp made her wince. She felt sick and dizzy and hopelessly alone. Too spent to argue or utter a word, she crept into her pyjamas with the help of Céline, who tucked her up in bed like a child.

'And now the warm drink,' she said briskly.

'How is the Comtesse this morning?' Sara queried, drinking the milk and wondering why her mother-in-law had not been in to see her.'

'The Comtesse left early this morning to spend the day with friends a short car run from here.'

Sara, trembling a little managed a stiff smile at Céline who was picking up her sodden garments and putting them into a neat pile. 'Is that wise? After all, she is not a hundred per cent fit. Did she leave early?'

'Before you were up, madame. You see, it is my day off duty and Madame, feeling as she does, decided to leave you and Monsieur Armand to spend the day together. In the circumstances perhaps I had better stay. I usually visit my parents, but if you need me. . . .'

Sara cut in hastily, for it was the last thing she wanted to have Céline or anyone stopping what she intended to do. 'No. It will not be necessary, thank you, Céline.' She paused, then plunged. 'Why did the Comtesse not tell me of her intention to spend the day out? Is she upset in any way?'

Céline folded the wet towel and placed it on top of the pile of clothes. 'The Comtesse is upset at your honeymoon being spoiled. *Les pauvres enfants*, she said to me this morning when I took her in an early breakfast, they are having a tough time of it one way or another, so I am going to give them a break. Tell Monsieur and Madame that I shall return late this evening and go right to bed.'

'Thank you for telling me, Céline. I shall be quite all right with Monsieur Armand, so enjoy your day out.'

Sara watched Céline leave with the pile of clothes and put down her empty cup. Lying back on her pillows, she closed her eyes, feeling desperately unhappy. What a mess she had made of everything. Poor Mistral! But she must not think of the mare because the tears . . . the tears. . . . The last thing she remembered was that Armand had drugged her drink.

The room was filled with shadows when she awoke, to find it was nine o'clock. Her head still felt muzzy, but the throbbing pains had gone. There was a hollow sensation in her stomach prompted by hunger, for she had not eaten all day, having missed her breakfast and lunch. All was silent with no sound coming from the next room, Armand's. Turning her head that way, she saw the covered tray on the table beside the bed. A savoury aroma was coming from it and the silver covered dishes were hot to the touch. Whoever had brought in the tray had awakened her. Her mouth twisted wryly. Armand had sent it up, of course, knowing she would not go down to dinner. But she was past eating.

Sara got up, reached for her empty cases and packed them determinedly. She had finished when the sound of a car arriving drew her to the window. It was her mother-in-law returning from her day out. Friends had brought her home, for she was having a word with them in the car before she left to go indoors. The car had halted just behind Armand's parked outside the front entrance. He had left it there in case of a hasty summons from Monsieur Ravel, presumably.

Conflicting ideas rushed through Sara's mind. There was nothing to stop her from taking Armand's car and driving to Paris where she could board a plane for London.

But she had forgotten one thing. Armand had her passport. She could search his room. It might just be in one of his suits in the wardrobe. He might carry it around in his day suit and not transfer it to his evening clothes when he changed. At the same time it occurred to her that he might still have it on him as he was unlikely to change for dinner on his own since his mother was out and she was in her room. Even so there was nothing to prevent her from searching his room, providing he was not there. So in her wrap and bare feet with her heart beating twenty to the dozen, Sara crept across her room and stealthily opened the communicating door.

The next moment her heart lurched. Armand was there. He sat in a chair with his arms along his knees and his head in his hands in silent despair. Tears rose unbidden as she witnessed his silent agony and felt his pain as if it was her own. What's happened to me? she asked herself wildly. The hate I had has gone. What I feel for him now is something more than just pity, much more. It's something which explains the anguished doubts, the sudden distortion of the Identi-kit picture I built up of him. To see him thus humbled when he had been so arrogant did not fill her with elation. His agony was like a huge hand squeezing her heart.

While Sara knew his pain was partly to do with the

terrible suspense of waiting to hear whether his father would live or die as a result of the drug, she also knew she was partly responsible for wounding him.

As if aware of her presence, he lifted his head and at the sight of the black hopelessness of his dark eyes in a ravaged face, Sara went swiftly across the room to draw his head against her.

His arms closed around her tightening painfully. 'Sara,' he groaned. 'Have you come to taunt me? Waiting today was bad enough, but the night will be never-ending.'

'No, not to taunt you, my dearest, only to comfort you.'

She ran her fingers through the crisp dark hair, wanting to tell him she would do anything in her power to ease his burden. It was not easy after the heartache of the past year – this decision to do something she might afterwards regret. But she loved him irrevocably and completely. There was no doubt about that. This wild coursing of her blood through her veins, this ecstatic feeling of suddenly coming to life with every fibre of her being in need of him was real and lasting.

When he pulled her down on to his lap to imprison her lips in an eternity of rapture, Sara slid her arms around his neck and drowned in pools of bliss. What joy to be her true self instead of acting a part! Armand released her at last to bury his face in her neck.

His voice was unusually thick. '*Chérie*,' he said humbly in a way which hurt her oddly, 'you are offering a little drink to a man dying of thirst. Take care. It is dangerous.'

Her blue eyes were both happy and bewildered. 'Armand, I . . .' she began, and got no further, for he was kissing her with an unleashed passion after days and nights of frustration. 'See what I mean?' He released her enough to look down at her, as breathless as she was. Tenderly he pushed the silken hair back from a face rosy from his kisses and held her blue eyes with his black ones. 'I despise myself for wanting you, for loving everything about you – your eyes, your hair, the beautiful way you walk, the warmth hidden beneath that hard core of revenge. Have you forgotten why you married me? Nothing has altered.'

Sara met his gaze fearlessly. 'I have altered, Armand. I love you, everything about you.'

'Everything?' he asked gravely.

A shadow flitted across her face. 'Everything,' she repeated.

He was looking down at her searchingly with a deep sadness in his eyes.

'How can you love me when you believe what you do about me?'

Her arms tightened round his neck. 'I've come to you when you have most need of me. Isn't that enough? Does it not prove my love?'

'Sara.' He spoke her name like a caress. 'If you loved me as I love you you would know I have had a desperate need of you since I met you and fell in love with you. Your giving yourself to me and my acceptance alters nothing, proves nothing. The way I feel tonight, any woman will suit my purpose in making me forget the agony of not knowing if my father will live. I am in hell.'

'Then let me share it with you,' she pleaded, turning her back on the heartbreaking past. 'Please, Armand.'

He had not put on a light and his eyes raked her face in the gloom. 'You mean just for tonight? Tomorrow you will prod at me again with some little new revenge. Is that it? I wonder if you know what true love means?'

Her lips trembled piteously. 'I love you so much that nothing else matters. It hurts inside me until I'm not myself any more but part of you.'

'You love me enough to forget the past, to take me on trust as I am, because that is what true love is all about?' he insisted with a hard deliberation. 'You believe your friend's death was no accident, that I in my way killed her. Can you forget that, put the past behind you and love me as I want to be loved?' He gave a sad smile which did not reach his eyes. 'Can you, *ma chère reine*?'

Tears came into her eyes at the old endearment she thought she would never hear again on his lips. The painful doubts would return, but she must never let him know nor even guess they were there. She had hurt him so much. 'Yes, yes,' she answered.

He looked down into her face for a long moment, his dark intent face undecided.

'Sara, I want to believe you. Somehow I feel there is a difference in you. I sensed it just now as if you loved me. It is true, is it not? You are not playing with me? For God's sake be honest!'

Her face mirrored the poignant entreaty coming from her heart. 'I do love you, Armand. I thought I hated you. When I came in the room just now I never meant it to be like this. I . . . I came to look for my passport. I was going to leave tonight, but when I saw you I knew I couldn't. I love you so much that your hurt is mine. My love for you is stronger than myself.' The tears rolled. 'You must believe me!'

He dealt with them gently. 'I believe you because you are the one woman I was created for. But if you have any doubts about my love tell me now. It will be too late afterwards for an annulment. You understand?'

She nodded solemnly, hurt by his tired eyes and the bitter pull of his mouth. I shall have to be careful what I say, she thought. I have to convince him of my sincerity and put the past behind me. Some day he will tell me the truth of what happened between Maura and himself. Until then I must not mention her again. Her smile was sweet and tender and there was no denying her love for him shining in her eyes.

Armand drew in a deep breath and with an incoherent exclamation bent his head to fasten his lips hungrily on hers. When his kiss deepened, Sara gave herself up to the ecstasy of it. His breathing quickened as his lips moved down to the hollow in her neck where he had bared her shoulder. Then, with her arms tight about his neck, he lifted her in his arms to carry her to their room.

# CHAPTER ELEVEN

THE next morning, Sara awakened in her bed with a difference. Armand was sleeping beside her with one arm flung across her. She snuggled down beside him, knowing that every moment he slept on was one less to wait in the ordeal of not knowing how his father was faring. Looking back, she realized how paltry her revenge had been. If only she had made him believe that she loved him! It was the only thing that mattered, and if they went on from there surely things would work out. How right Julian had been when he had suggested them leading separate lives in order for her to have the chance of settling down with some one. Sara had never realized what heaven it was to live with a man. She rued bitterly the limitations of her mind – a mind obsessed with revenge.

She shivered at the thought of how easily she could have lost Armand. Together they had discovered the unending joy in the intimacy of belonging. She closed her eyes, remembering her own gentleness responding to his. She opened them again to find Armand looking at her so intently that the soft colour flooded her cheeks. He chuckled and drew her against him.

'Was it frightening, *ma pauvre enfant*, to love a man you knew practically nothing about?' he whispered, breathing in the fragrance of her hair.

'It was heaven, Armand,' she answered against his brown throat. 'At the same time it frightens me, this love I have for you. It is bigger than life.'

'You have no cause to be afraid, *ma chère reine. . . .*' He paused and she lifted her eyes to see the gleam in his and the hard set of his jaw. 'Unless you ever try to leave me. Then you will really be in trouble. You will discover the devil in me which can be roused when my possessions are threatened.'

Her eyes did not flinch. 'I'm not afraid of that. I'm yours for as long as you want me.' She hesitated, but the urge to speak out and destroy for ever the barrier between them was too great to be ignored. 'You do believe I love you and that I'm truly sorry for what I did to Mistral? I didn't mean to hurt her.' She blinked back the tears. 'She would have been alive today if I hadn't taken her out.'

'Mistral had lived her life. The vet said her heart would give out at any time. She died in action as she would have wished.'

'And you haven't stopped loving me?'

'*Mignonne*, I never stopped loving you. You cannot stop loving a person who is your whole life. I admit I was furious on our wedding night when you told me a few home truths, and I was hurt as only a man can be hurt by the woman he loves. But I soon lost my anger. I began to hope that given time my love would find an answering chord in you. We are so right for each other, both physically and mentally. You had to love me. And there had to be trust with that love.'

'There is.' Sara looked at him with swimming blue eyes. 'I must have loved you from the start, but I wouldn't admit it.'

Their kiss was one of passion and understanding. Presently Armand almost groaned as he pressed his hard cheek against her soft one. 'The time we have wasted!'

'I'll make it up to you, darling,' she said, stroking the lean hard jaw.

They were late going down to breakfast and met the Comtesse leaving her room.

'*Bonjour, mes enfants,*' she cried, looking shrewdly at Sara, who shone with a new radiance. 'Being together suits you. How happy you look!'

Armand chuckled and bent to kiss his mother's cheek. 'We intend to do it more often. Are you having breakfast with us?'

His mother smiled teasingly. 'Shall I be in the way?'

'We can put up with it,' Armand smiled wickedly.

'Of course you won't be in the way,' Sara stated firmly.

No mention of Mistral was made during that gay meal with Armand assuming a teasing front. Sara knew it was put on for his mother's benefit. Céline must not have mentioned the incident with Mistral to her mistress. She had obviously been well trained. It was Armand who mentioned it as casually as he was able.

Mistral died yesterday, Maman – from a heart attack.'

He spoke quietly and Sara felt his hurt deeply. She would have given anything to recall the happenings of the previous day leading to Mistral's collapse. Sara looked at his dark handsome features which were somehow not swarthy; the black eyes; the tousled hair. There was a latent strength in his splendid physique, but he looked tired and lean – too lean.

Tears sprang to the hazel eyes of the Comtesse. 'Poor Mistral! Of course, we knew she would not last for ever. When did it happen?'

'Yesterday. She was out at the time.'

His mother's eyes widened and she gave a sad smile. 'But surely that is the way she would have wished to go. She loved to be out, and storms never bothered her.'

Sara could not meet Armand's eyes. But how relieved she was to hear the words of comfort from his mother. She was about to admit that it was her fault when a man-servant came to tell Armand he was wanted on the phone in the hall. She did meet his eyes then to give him a reassuring smile. He smiled back, but his eyes were grave and he looked strangely pale. The Comtesse, sublimely unaware of the gravity of the phone call, was replenishing her coffee cup and did not notice her son's tenseness as he left the room.

He seemed to be away a very long time and Sara was left to a spate of introspection in between talking to the Comtesse. She had imagined love to be a wild exciting feeling tempered by security – a wonderful sensation of belonging – of never having again to walk alone. In Armand's arms she had felt the happiness it could bring. Away from them she only knew the sweet tormenting torture of giving her heart into the keeping of a loved one whose confidence was not wholly hers. Yet however much you loved someone you would never know their inmost feelings or thoughts. She loved him more than life, but would the little nagging doubt of him eventually prick the bubble of her happiness? She might even grow to hate him again because of her belief that he had let Maura down and thus caused her death. She had given him her word that she loved him above all that nothing mattered except their love for each other. But it did matter. Even if the miracle she was praying for happened and his father was spared, even though Armand never alluded to or gave another thought to her tragic beliefs, the fear would always be there. There was no hope of her finding lasting happiness until she knew the truth.

The click of the door opening brought her back to her surroundings. Armand strode in smiling. 'Wonderful news!' he said. 'Papa is much better. The drug Ravel used is an unqualified success. All trace of the sleeping sickness has gone. He is himself again!'

The Comtesse was crying quietly and Armand was behind her chair. 'You have yet to hear the rest of my news,' he whispered in her ear. 'He is coming home tomorrow. Ravel is coming with him for a day or so to keep an eye on his progress, and to continue with his treatment.'

His mother dabbed hastily at her eyes. 'I'm sorry for making a scene, but I am so happy.'

'Of course you are, *ma petite*. We all are.' He cast a mocking look across the table at Sara. 'Your daughter-in-law is crying too.'

And so she was, blinking back the tears. They had to laugh then. Armand was still standing behind his mother's chair looking at Sara when he said, 'I shall not be here when Papa returns home tomorrow. I have to go away.'

'Why, Armand? Surely not at a time like this?' his mother cried in dismay.

'I am afraid I have to. That was why I was so long on the phone. I had to ring up the office this morning. I am to report there in three hours' time. I have to go abroad for a few days.'

'Abroad?' Sara echoed. The dismay she felt at his

words was on her face. She wanted to ask him to take her with him, tell him that she was only strong when he was there with his strength.

'It will only be a matter of a few days,' he said gently, his dark eyes holding hers reassuringly.

With inward disquiet, Sara watched his mother twist in her chair to look up at him. 'Is it dangerous, this assignment?'

He shrugged carelessly. 'No more dangerous than everyday life in the crowded city.'

'Poor Sara,' was her comment. 'What a honeymoon!'

'I am afraid Maman is disgusted at the way our honeymoon is being interrupted,' he said when the Comtesse had left them together. 'Are you disappointed too, *mignonne*?'

Sara swallowed painfully as the feel of his arms about her told her how much she longed for him. She wanted to put her head on his shoulder and forget everything but the joy of being with him. If only she could think that Maura would be glad of their belonging! If only Mistral was alive. If only she had not married him in a spirit of revenge. There were so many ifs.

She shook her head and smiled wanly, neither resisting nor surrendering to his embrace I'll bear it knowing you have forgiven me about Mistral and. . . .'

He cut in, feeling her withdrawal from his arms. 'All that is over and done with, almost,' he said roughly.

'Almost?' she repeated quickly. 'What do you mean?'

'Forget it!' Suddenly he was gripping her shoulders, holding them so hard that she could have winced with the pain of it. 'What I want is to be sure of your love for me in face of everything that has gone before. I want you to love me and to trust me.'

'I love you and I trust you,' she told him, rashly following the dictates of her heart. It was the truth, but she wished she could feel more happy about it.

He gave her that charming smile which brightened his sardonic face. 'That is what I wanted to hear.' And then, serious again, 'Not regretting last night, are you, *chérie*?'

'How could I? Our love for each other is the most wonderful thing that has ever happened to me.'

'*Mignonne!*' He drew her against his heart, bending to kiss her lips tenderly. 'We are going to be wildly, gloriously happy. And do not imagine our married life is going to be like this with me kissing you good-bye at intervals to leave you to go on some mission. This is my last assignment. I am leaving the Foreign Service.'

Sara looked up at him with fear in her eyes. 'Then it is dangerous, this work you do?'

'Shall we say it is a challenge and an exciting life for a single man but not for a married one. I wonder now why I refused to join my father when he offered me a partnership on the estate, unless it was to prove I could carve out my own career independent of my family.' He looked down searchingly into her face. 'Will you mind having a farmer for a husband?'

Fleetingly, Sara dwelt on the extracts from Maura's letters, his wild parties, moonlight bathing, his love of city life. The pain inside her did not blind her to the purposefulness behind his surface gaiety. She knew he was capable of disciplining himself to take whatever path he chose and adhere to it. But remembered pain brought niggling doubts as she knew it would. Her look was just as searching.

'You won't be bored in rural surroundings after city life?' she asked.

'Why on earth should I? I was brought up at the Chateau and I loved it. When one lives in the city one has to conform to pattern or be miserable. But in the country there are other distractions much more exciting – when one has a wife especially.' His black eyes twinkled devilishly. 'And we have a lot of loving to make up for time lost.'

He laughed at the wild rose colour flooding her face. Then he sobered to draw her against him a little roughly. 'How am I going to survive without you?' An ardent five minutes passed given to caresses and kisses, then, 'You will be all right with my parents until I return.' He was looking down at her now broodingly. 'And go easy with

Ravel. While I am grateful to him for what he has done for Papa I have no intention of encouraging his friendship with my wife. Always remember, *mignonne*, that I love you now and for ever and that you and I are already one.'

And Sara had to agree, knowing that these precious moments borrowed from time were only too fleeting.

The Comte came home the following day. Monsieur Ravel travelled behind the ambulance in his car. The Chateau was a hive of activity and well lit with smiles all round. Everyone was pleased to have the beloved Comte back home again.

Sara did not see him on that first day. The journey had exhausted him and Monsieur Ravel had given him a sedative so that he slept most of the time. His wife was in and out of his room, and Sara was moved to tears at her obvious delight at having her beloved husband back home and on the road to recovery. Friends rang up and endless flowers, fruit and small gifts kept arriving all day.

'So you have lost your husband in the line of duty,' Ravel said, strolling beside Sara that evening in the grounds after dinner.

The Comtesse, like a mother with a new baby, had gone to take a peep at her husband to see if he was all right. Sara longed to ask this dependable silent man about Armand. Yet what could she say? Not much unless she wanted to give the situation away. He had a keen perception and would probably read between the lines of anything she asked him. In the end, Sara decided against it.

'Yes,' she replied laconically.

It was a perfect evening for a walk outdoors and Sara knew by heart the turns and twists of the paths in the beautiful gardens escorting her willing companion along a path near a high stone wall thickly covered with vines of golden and purple grapes. There was a carved seat near and she sat down upon it, spreading out her dress. Monsieur Ravel dropped beside her. He leaned back with a sigh revelling in the quiet beauty of the night and breathed in deeply of the nocturnal scents coming from lawns and flower beds.

'Cigarette?' he asked, producing his case.

'Not just now. But you smoke.' She watched him select a cigarette and light it admiring his square capable hands. It occurred to her that he wore his clothes well and he was not without a certain amount of charm and fascination. 'Why is it,' she murmured, 'that Frenchmen are so fascinating?'

He raised somewhat rough brows and laughed, giving her an appraising but wary look. 'Don't tell me that I am in that category of charming Frenchman!'

'I'm not only telling you, you are. At least, I think so.'

His regard now held a sharpness in its depth. They were sitting in the pathway of light from a newly risen moon. Her skin had a pearly texture, her clear eyes were deep blue jewels of light and her mouth was sweetly curved, enchantingly if she but knew it.

'You are very sweet,' was the quiet rejoinder. 'You are very much in the minority in your opinion of my charms. But you have made my day.'

'You are much too modest, like all great men. I would like to thank you for what you have done for Armand's father. It's like a miracle. It must have been an ordeal for you too waiting for the result. I know surgeons don't enjoy risking a failure because of the harm it does to their reputation, which is why I admire you so much.'

'In a case like the Comte's where the utmost speed was essential the risk had to be taken. This is one of those times when I feel it is worth all the hard work, the disappointments and the heart aches my job entails. Did you know Armand called in to see his father at the hospital before he left for abroad?'

'No, but I expected him to.'

'I am fond of Armand, and while he is lucky to have so charming a wife, you are lucky too. He is a man any man would be proud to have for his friend.'

Sara was surprised at the calmness of her voice when, after a hardly perceptible pause, she answered, 'I should imagine he would say the same about you.'

He gave her another appraising glance, then blew out a veil of smoke. 'We are good friends, and I am very happy to know he has a wife whom it will give me the greatest pleasure to call my friend also. You will find life quiet here after London?'

Sara did not answer for a moment or so. He had the same idea as her mother-in-law of her becoming bored with rural life. Yet she would have said it was Armand they had to worry about. He was the gay one. If only she could get at the truth, persuade him to reveal all that she was sure lay in his mind. She had come very near to it when he had kissed her good-bye, but the truth still eluded her.

With an effort, Sara dragged her mind back to the present and the man beside her and told him a little of her early life. He was immensely interested to hear of her show-jumping successes, being a keen rider himself. And when they finally made their way back to the Chateau, Sara felt she had made a friend.

After an early morning ride on Mimi during which she was accompanied by Claude Ravel, Sara had breakfast, then went to see the Comte. With the smiling Comtesse she entered the now familiar lovely room to see the Comte occupying his half of the big bed. He was so much like Armand that she felt an anguished pull on her heart-strings. In the silk pyjamas, his wide-shouldered frame suggested a splendid physique and there was more black than grey in the thick unruly hair. Though the sallowness of his face made it appear long and narrow, the black eyes twinkled devilishly. Sara thought, the potent family charm was as intoxicating as the wine they had made famous throughout the years.

When the Comtesse had introduced her, Sara did something which surprised even herself. Bending her head, she kissed the gaunt cheek. 'May I say how very happy I am to see you back home again,' she said a little huskily.

'*Merci*, Sara.' Henri Romond de Poulain looked with appraisal at the flushed cheeks, the shy deepening blue of her eyes and the smooth pale gold hair. 'I could not have chosen better myself,' was his verdict.

'Exactly what I thought,' admitted his wife, putting an arm around Sara's slim waist. 'We have much to make up for to Sara, *chérie*. So far her honeymoon has been more or less without a bridegroom.'

'So I understand,' was the Comte's grave reply. He made a gesture of irritation with an emaciated hand. 'What is this assignment Armand has undertaken? I'll never know why on earth he did not go into partnership with me years ago when I first suggested it instead of careering all over the universe on these secret missions. He came to see me yesterday before he left, but he was not allowed to stay long enough for us to talk. And I must confess I did not feel up to it.' Exhausted, he lay back against his pillows as if the sudden spurt of disapproval of his son's actions had taken all his strength. Claude Ravel entered then as if on cue and they exchanged a few pleasantries. The surgeon was evidently pleased with his patient's progress and Sara left the room considerably cheered about it but very perturbed about his son.

For the rest of the day she tried to close her mind against the thought immediately taking possession of it at the Comte's reference to the secret mission being undertaken by Armand. She felt stricken at the thought that it could be dangerous. Yet if it were, surely Armand would have told her about his affair with Maura in order to clear himself in case he did not return. Or did he regard his silence as being a sure test of her love and faith in him? While her brain told her he was being unfair to keep her in ignorance of the facts, her heart concentrated upon the appalling, frightening thought of his never returning.

Sara had known that life would be meaningless without him with every waking thought a torment of hopeless longing. And it was worse than she had ever imagined. She had to admit how wrong she had been to ever think she could leave him, despite the heartbreaking memory of Maura, who would always prevent her from having peace of mind. Armand had proved his point anyway. I love him more than life, she thought despairingly, and despised herself for wanting him on any terms.

During the next few days, Sara was thankful for the companionship of Claude Ravel. They went riding together every day, played tennis on the hard courts of the Chateau and went for walks in the grounds. The Comtesse spent most of her time with her husband, who was making excellent progress. Things had never been dull since his arrival at the Chateau and suddenly social life became the order of the day. There was an immediate influx of presents for the invalid, baskets of fruit, books, delicacies and flowers followed eventually by the senders in person.

When Claude Ravel left after a satisfying surveillance of the Comte, Sara found herself more or less with her own thoughts for company, and she had no heart for meeting the innumerable visitors to the Chateau. The constant effort of having to keep a bright front was beginning to be very wearing in the face of her fears for Armand's safety. He had been gone nearly a week with no word, and though she realized the nature of his work might prevent him from communicating with her, it did not help.

Sara looked forward to her daily rides on Mimi. Mistral's box was now occupied by an Arab stallion, but Sara could never pass it without thinking about the horse Armand had loved so much. Her rides on the estate were entirely without incident. The only people she met were the workers going about on their daily tasks. So she was surprised one morning to see a rider coming towards her as she skirted the woods.

He was a young man of twenty-five or so, clean-shaven, blond with rather small brown eyes and the rather long nose of his Norman ancestors. He rode superbly, his bright hair gleaming in the sun as a lock of it fell tantalizingly on his forehead. He reined in just ahead of her looking her over with appraisal with an impudent smile on his face. The smile dissolved the weak line of his jaw, tightening his sensuous mouth, and Sara found him extremely attractive and likeable.

'*Bonjour, madame,*' he greeted her in English. 'They

say the early bird catches the worm. I am indeed favoured this morning, if you will forgive the trite simile.'

He spoke in a cultured voice and held his slightly built figure proudly. Instantly there was a quality of silence between them, brief but tangible; a quality of apprehension, so fleeting that moments later Sara was wondering if she had imagined it. Certainly there had been no surprise on his face at their meeting and he had called her Madame. Yet Sara had to smile. His bantering air, though a trifle bold for a complete stranger, was refreshing.

'*Bonjour, monsieur*,' she answered warily. 'Are you not trespassing on private property?'

He gave an exaggerated bow of French gallantry and lifted his head proudly.

'My mother, the Comtesse d'Edard, is sister to the Comte Romond de Poulain. Armand and I are cousins.' His smile flashed. 'You may call me Beau, cousin.'

For some inexplicable reason his manner grated. Sara could not have explained why she found herself resenting him and his manner of approach. A lack of respect – that was it. For while he made her aware of herself as a woman and a very attractive one, he also gave her the feeling that he regarded her sex as negligible. Reluctant to continue the conversation with him, Sara moved Mimi on and found him riding beside her. A member of the Romond de Poulain family he might be, but he had none of their endearing qualities of being gentle and courteous and admirably considerate towards their staff. Sara could not imagine this young man being considerate towards anyone except for his own ends.

Curiosity prompted her to ask, 'How did you know who I was?'

'I heard that my cousin Armand had acquired a beautiful wife and a magnificent stallion. I decided to ride over to see them.'

Sara gave a wry smile. 'Just like that,' she said sweetly. He really was an insufferable, conceited and malicious young man, with an obvious chip on his shoulder. 'You make it sound as though I had been purchased as an appendage to the household!'

'Everyone has his price,' he said insolently.

It was a remark to whip the colour to her cheeks and the sparks to her eyes.

'Indeed? Then I would say you certainly would not amount to much – not in my estimation. *Bonjour, monsieur.*'

Sara urged Mimi forward into a gallop, holding on to the remnants of her temper.

What an odious young man he was, with the sting of a scorpion! Mimi went like the wind, but his horse was more powerful and stronger. He soon overtook her. Reaching out for Mimi's bridle to bring her alongside, he apologized.

'I am afraid it was jealousy. I have always been jealous of Armand. Why did you have to be so enchanting?'

'Enchanting?' she echoed, allowing her horse to settle into a trot beside him. 'I am only very ordinary.'

'I repeat, you are enchanting, and I am eaten up with jealousy. Here was I hoping you would be some shrew who would give Armand hell.'

Sara's sudden laughter was unaffected and delightful. 'You're behaving like a spoilt child. Jealousy will get you nowhere. Are you married?'

'*Mon dieu*, no!'

He would not be, of course. Sara could not see him shackled with all the responsibility and deep emotions marriage incurred. 'Why so vehement about it? You appear to be jealous of your cousin's marriage.'

'No, only of his bride. I do not think I will go to see the stallion after all. It is sure to be as perfect as you.'

'Surely that is the attitude of a defeatist? What's to prevent you marrying some girl far more lovely than I am or buying a stallion?'

His short laugh was derisive. 'Chance is a fine thing, the cash is another.'

'If you're short of cash surely you can work for it. Have you a job?'

'Not at the moment. I have a surfeit of gambling

debts.' He quirked a thoughtful eyebrow. 'You do not happen to have plenty of cash, I suppose?'

Sara laughed again. 'Not that kind. You're not in trouble, are you?'

His shrug was very French. 'I have been in worse.'

'Why so despondent? A moment ago you were riding high.'

'You remind me of something I wish to forget.'

'I do?'

'Forget it. See you tomorrow, probably. *Au revoir*.'

He went with a wave of the hand, leaving Sara to finish her ride alone. Strange, Armand not inviting him to the wedding if he was a cousin, she mused, then promptly forgot about him when she arrived back at the Chateau to see if there was any mail from Armand.

# CHAPTER TWELVE

Sara did not go for an early morning ride the next day. The Comtesse, perturbed about her being so much on her own, had taken her out to dine with friends and they had been late returning to the Chateau. The result was that Sara overslept and stayed indoors to wait for the early morning post in case there was a letter from Armand. It was also the day fires were lighted in the Petit Chateau and she had a yearning to pay another visit there.

There was no post for her and, swallowing her disappointment, Sara walked through the grounds to the Petit Chateau carrying a long flower basket filled with blooms to place in the rooms. A log fire already burned in the hall and Sara entered with a feeling of coming home. Once again she delighted in the lofty elegant rooms with their beautifully moulded double doors leading to each room.

Lovingly she arranged the flowers in vases and bowls and watered the many potted plants so loved by the French. What doubts she had about living in the Chateau were charmed away by the happy atmosphere she felt pervading every room. And she returned across the beautiful grounds feeling much brighter. Yet she would have been happy with Armand in a garret. She missed him more as the days went by with no word from him.

In her longing for him Sara began to realize how little material things mattered; how much time she had wasted in dwelling on the past. If only Armand would return! Since her meeting with his cousin Beau that morning, Sara's thoughts had been centred on both men, comparing Armand's strong jaw and firm mouth with Beau's sensuous lips and weak chin – Armand's black eyes, widely spaced, both piercing and intelligent directed upon her with a fearless intent with Beau's surreptitious glances from small eyes too closely set. Beau might be the younger of the two men, but it was he who had the jaded look of too many late nights and too much love of the clandestine kind. Sara blushed at her own deduction of a man she knew practically nothing about but who in her opinion had every appearance of the dissolute. Would to heaven she knew the truth about Armand!

She lunched alone. The Comtesse was out shopping and having her hair done for the small dinner party to be given that evening at the Chateau, her first since her husband's illness. He had been coming down to lunch each day, resting during the afternoon and coming down to dine in the evenings. Today he was having lunch in his room conserving his strength for the dinner party that evening.

Ravel had paid a flying visit during the week, delighted with his patient's progress. There had been no return of the fever or the sleepy sickness and the Comte's recovery, backed by his strong constitution, had been nothing short of miraculous.

According to the Comtesse there would only be a chosen few for dinner, very close friends and relations. Later, when the Comte was better, they would be entertaining again on the grand scale to which they were accustomed. But Sara was not looking forward to the party and she dressed with some trepidation with a longing for Armand to be by her side on such an occasion.

She had elected to wear the white dress with its scooped-out neckline, knowing it would look well with the sapphire necklace and matching ear-rings. Céline had brushed her pale gold hair until it shone and twisted it into thick gleaming coils on the top of her small head. The result was enchanting, for the thought of being the cynosure of all eyes, the butt of whispers of approval or disapproval, had brought flags of colour to Sara's cheeks and her blue eyes were no less brilliant than the sparkling necklace around her slender throat.

'Parfait!' the Comtesse exclaimed when Sara joined her in-laws to greet their guests. 'How beautiful you look, chérie. Does she not, Henri?'

'Enchanté.' The Comte bent low in teasing tribute. He was looking very distinguished in evening dress, a little gaunt but still handsome.

Their kindness as always touched an answering chord in Sara's heart as they drew her into the family circle and made her feel completely at home. She had experienced a sense of belonging from the day of her arrival at the Chateau and now she had the feeling of being there for years. Thanks to the Comtesse, she thought, who was looking exquisite in an evening dress in a soft shade of lilac. Her antique necklace, beautiful in colour and design, reflected the colour of her dress in the brilliant stones and Sara realized how lovely she really was. She was happy this evening with her beloved husband at her side as he introduced Sara to their guests.

In the charmingly decorated hall among flower arrangements beneath the golden glow of crystal chandeliers, Sara met many delightful people, some of them titled, and gave a conventional smile. Dinner had been announced and they were drifting into the dining-room when Beau arrived. Sara had not heard him announced and she watched him advance swiftly and politely towards them, wishing she had found time to tell her mother-in-law of her meeting with him the previous morning.

The Comte's introduction was brief and a little curt. Beau was very late and she had the idea that he had been assigned as her escort for the evening.

'Sara, my nephew Beau, who is rather late as an escort.' The Comte's words confirmed Sara's thoughts. 'Beau – Sara, Armand's wife, whom I believe you have not met.'

Beau, unperturbed, bestowed a smile both friendly and warm upon Sara, who was suddenly aware of his charm, not the real irresistable charm giving one an assurance of an underlying sincerity but the surface charm of a vivid personality.

He acknowledged the introduction with the aplomb of a perfect stranger and offered Sara his arm with French gallantry to lead her to the dining-room. Moved by his friendly greeting, she was disturbed by conflicting emotions as he seated her at the dining-table before lowering himself beside her. She was finding it difficult not to like him in spite of the fact of his not mentioning the fact that they had already met.

It was not really important, she argued, and resigned herself to the pleasure of his company. At least she felt at ease with him, which was more than she would have felt seated by some stranger. She turned gratefully towards him, to find him watching her with those small eyes which seemed to miss nothing. And from then on he set out to amuse her. He proved to be extremely entertaining but did not take kindly to her amusement when he attempted to flirt with her.

'Come out into the grounds,' he said when everyone made a move to leave the dining-room much later.

Sara walked beside him wishing he were Armand. The moon-filled grounds fading into neutrality, the brilliant colours of exotic blooms, mocked at her loneliness. She was discovering agonizingly just how empty life could be without her laconic, black-eyed husband. He was in her blood like rich red corpuscles enriching her life and without which she would die. Torture without him and torture with him because she did not really know him.

'Where is the bridegroom?' Beau asked without preamble or apology.

Sara, startled at his true reading of her thoughts, replied after a brief pause:

'Away on business.'

He cocked an inquiring brow in her direction. 'Brief courtship, briefer honeymoon,' he commented dryly. 'Do you not mind being left so precipitately?'

'He had no choice,' she told him swiftly. 'It has to do with his job before we were married.'

'I have to hand it to him,' her companion admitted half involuntarily. 'He is the most versatile man I know. I am a little inclined that way myself, though for a less worthier cause. I play the casino in the winter and the racecourse in the summer, with a tinkle of night life and women sandwiched somewhere in between.'

Sara had the uneasy feeling of continuing a dangerous conversation, when she asked, 'Were you surprised to hear of Armand's marriage?'

'Rather. While to me he has always appeared to be reserved with women, I know he is a man of experience with them. He also has deep capabilities of feeling and passion, but how far he allows himself to go is anybody's guess. Women have always found him attractive, but he has never allowed them to clutter up his life as I have done. But then I do not possess his will power.'

'Why envy him it? Why not cultivate your own? You can give Armand a few years. There's nothing to stop you from being yourself.'

'I have never been allowed to be myself from the day I was born. It has always been,' and here he mimicked, ' "Why cannot you be more like Armand?" '

Sara smiled – she had to. 'Having someone to live up to can be very wearing, I'm sure, especially when you want to waste your own talents in a life of ease.'

'Not trying to reform me by any chance, are you?'

They had reached a garden seat and Sara sat down. 'I would be spoiling your fun, would I not, if I did? What about your parents?'

'Dead. Killed in a car crash not long ago.'

'I'm sorry,' she said.

He sat down beside her to contemplate her quizzically. 'Sorry I have lost my parents or sorry for me for what I am?'

'Both. I'm sure you would be happier doing something more worthwhile.'

'Unfortunately the leopard cannot change its spots.'

'I think they're spots you have given yourself,' Sara said with a prompt and easy comradeship. 'You could easily replace them with stripes if you wished.'

Beau pushed his hands into his pockets and stretched his legs out before him.

'Like the tiger I was named after?' he mocked.

Sara went cold. Her heart missed a beat, then thundered on. 'I don't understand. I didn't know you were named after someone.'

He looked startled. 'You have not been told that I was named after my beloved cousin Armand? Beau is the name the family use in order not to confuse us.' His tone was bitter, but Sara had the feeling that Armand was not responsible for all the bitterness. She was thinking something else too, something which made her feel sick with a blow as it was below the belt. If what she was thinking was true.

She moistened dry lips. 'Have you ever worked at the British Embassy in Paris?'

'Did Armand tell you he used his influence to get me a job there? I lasted four months.'

'Armand told me nothing. I had a friend worked there not long ago – Maura Penhurst. Did you know her?'

There was a pause during which Sara felt her heart thudding enough to knock a hole in her ribs.

'Yes, I knew her.' No more.

Four words which told Sara the shattering truth. Unsteadily, she rose to her feet, hardly aware of her lips moving. 'She was my best friend.'

She had to leave him then to run wildly through the grounds as yet empty of other guests. To avoid meeting any of them, her flying feet carried her around the back of the house where it was possible to reach the hall via a long corridor past the kitchen quarters. Luck was with her, for she gained the foot of the stairs meeting no one. Then, looking up, her heart dropped to see the Comtesse descending them.

'Sara!' she cried, and regarded her searchingly. 'You are out of breath and you are quite pale. I suppose you have come in for your wrap. I saw you going out into the grounds with Beau and I wondered whether to send Céline up for it. I know you young things do not feel the cold so much, but I was rather concerned.' She reached the foot of the stairs to where Sara stood as though glued to the spot and patted her arm. 'We must look after you or we shall have Armand to reckon with! Do not stay out too long.'

Sara managed a smile and leaned forward to kiss her mother-in-law's perfumed cheek before running up the stairs. Once in her room she sank into the nearest chair like an inflated balloon. She still could not believe that it must have been Beau and not Armand who had played fast and loose with Maura. Her hands cupped her face in horror. She had taken her revenge on an innocent man. How could she ever have thought Armand guilty of such conduct? She must have been out of her mind. If only she had known the existence of another Armand in the diplomatic service what torture she would have been spared! Bitterly it came to her that her marriage would then have been the real thing from the beginning and not the sham it had started out to be. Armand would have changed her opinion of Frenchmen and eventually had her surrendering ecstatically to his masterful wooing. But that last letter from Maura had changed everything. Armand had wanted her to love him wholeheartedly despite what she had believed. Well, she did, and her love had brought him nothing but pain, because it had its roots in revenge.

How could she face him again, knowing the truth? The utter relief of knowing Armand innocent of the charges she had nurtured against him was forgotten in the knowledge that she had hurt him so badly and taken her marriage vows in bitterness and hate.

As she sat there her emotions simmered down to a deadly calm. The show had to go on. The party was a happy one and it was up to her not to spoil it. She went downstairs. Beau must have left early, for she did not see him again, and somehow she got through the rest of the evening.

It had rained during the night and the early morning air was fresh with the tang of damp earth and sweetened with honeysuckle and wild rose. Mimi's hooves sent up a smell of crushed grass and Sara closed her eyes, revelling in the peace and loveliness of her surroundings. No hedges closed in the fields of the estate, but there were sturdy ancient trees with magnificent foliage, giving shade to the workers on the land when they stopped for refreshment.

Sara reined Mimi in at the top of the hill behind the Chateau outside the circle of magnificent chestnut trees which encircled the Chateau and swept on down the driveway to the wrought iron entrance gates. Shadowy hills were becoming more defined in the gathering strength of the morning light, flowers were beginning to lift their heads to greet the lazy sun and birds twittered in the trees.

Sara had spent a restless night and had taken the early morning ride to refresh her mind. It had occurred to her during her tossing and turning in the dark hours that she should have stayed with Beau to talk about Maura. Had she not been so upset she would have done. It was too late now. Suddenly, the rhythmic dull thud of hooves on the damp ground made her turn her head sharply to see the object of her thoughts riding towards her.

'You are out early.' Sara's greeting was cool as he reined in his horse a few feet away.

He looked pale and drawn as if he had not slept too well himself and he spoke jerkily. 'Why did you end our conversation so abruptly last evening by running away?'

Sara, thinking fleetingly of Maura, hardened her heart. 'Perhaps I hadn't the stomach for it,' she replied coldly. 'But I would like to talk to you about Maura if you don't mind.'

He shot her a keen glance. 'Shall we ride?'

Sara nodded and turned Mimi away from the circle of chestnut trees to face the open fields, then slowed her down to walking pace.

Beau, following her lead, drew in beside her and did the same. Then, clearing his throat nervously, he began:

'I met Maura for the first time one morning in Paris riding through the Bois. Her skill in handling her mount and the fact that she was English intrigued me. She rode superbly, her cheeks glowed with the wind and her hair was blown into a profusion of curls. It occurred to me then how very attractive and stimulating she was in an exciting way. We got talking, and when we discovered we both worked at the British Embassy we lunched there together every day. Soon she was caught up in the gay crowd I went around with, and I set out to give her a good time.'

'Maura wrote to me about you,' Sara told him without expression. 'She was in love with you.' She paused, wondering how much to tell him and how much he knew about Maura's tragic end.

'I know,' he said. 'We now come to the night of the party given for Maura. I had come here to fetch my parents. I had told them of my intention to ask Maura to be my wife and they had consented to go to the party to meet her. To be honest I had no intention of marrying Maura or anyone else until I found I could not stand the thought of her leaving to go back to London.' He gave a bitter laugh. 'I even bought a ring! Everything went wrong that night. To begin with we were late starting back to Paris. It was raining heavily and the roads merited careful driving. But I was in a hurry because I had not told Maura of my intentions. I meant to surprise her with the ring, and my parents. We never reached the party. We crashed into a wall just outside Paris. I came to in hospital hours later lucky to escape with bruises and a slight concussion. Knowing that the party would be over, I asked a nurse to ring Maura at her flat. There was no reply. The next morning I was told she was dead and that my parents had been killed instantly in the car crash.'

Tears were rolling down Sara's cheeks unashamedly. 'I'm sorry. What rotten luck!' It was too late to know how wrong she had been in mixing up past life with the future. Sara swallowed on the futility of it and decided to say nothing that might add to her companion's remorse.

Nothing much passed between them for the rest of the ride. Beau was too preoccupied with his thoughts and Sara could not define her feelings at all. They were all too mixed up. Beau's account of what really happened on the night Maura had died was even more shattering than the thought of what she had done to Armand, her husband. Would he ever really forgive her in his heart? Would not the memory of it always be between them? She found herself longing for the comfort of his presence and at the same time dreading meeting him again. What a mess everything was. What was she going to say to a husband who held her heart in his strong brown hands? And so

173

Sara tormented herself as she returned to the Chateau to put a brave face on for the benefit of her in-laws.

After breakfast the weather changed. The sky became leaden and towards lunch the rain pelted down. Sara spent the morning helping the Comte to catch up with his correspondence. They had become firm friends and she enjoyed every moment she spent in his company. He was so happy to know that Armand was going to help in the running of the estate and Sara knew the thought was a great incentive to him getting well.

The rain certainly did not keep visitors away, for they arrived in their cars at intervals during the day, keeping the Comtesse on her toes. In the afternoon, Sara helped to entertain them. Towards the evening as they waved off the last of the visitors, the rain stopped and the storm clouds rolled away, leaving the air still oppressive and to Sara vaguely full of foreboding.

There were to be no guests for dinner that evening. The Comtesse very sensibly decided not to have a surfeit of dinner parties until her husband was a hundred per cent fit again. Before preparing for dinner, Sara spent some time at her room window gazing out at a newly washed world. She would have given anything to have gone for a short canter on Mimi to rid herself of a depressed feeling which had persisted all day since her meeting with Beau that morning. She had intended to tell the Comtesse about him, but there had not been time or opportunity to do so. Her compassion urged her to find out more about him, who he lived with and if there was anything she could do to help him. There was so much she did not know – for instance, what Armand thought about him. Thinking about Armand made her realize how very wearing it was trying to keep up a bright front with the knowledge of not being able to uphold it indefinitely.

She was turning from the window when the sound of car wheels crunching on gravel and the shriek of brakes swung her back to look down on the drive below. A car door slammed and Sara had a glimpse of Armand's wide shoulders and dark head as he strode into the Chateau.

Sara's deep breath was brought on by a swift sense of shock. Her sudden reaction – one of panic – took her as far as the door which she opened quietly to hear Armand in the hall below greeting Raoul and asking questions. They were joined by the Comtesse and her voice pitched on a happy tone drew nearer. Then a door closed and all was silent. By this time Sara was shaking violently with a closed fist pressed against her mouth. How could she meet those fine dark eyes and see in them what a fool she had been? She knew a deep shame in treating him so disgracefully – degraded and self-contemptuous. Gradually her panic died and the tears came and with the tears a choking sensation of being in a confined space. The walls seemed to be closing in on her. She had to get out.

Bewildered and desperately unhappy, she ran downstairs and out into the sweet night air to look around her like a hunted deer. She was crying quietly now and hurrying on in case she was seen. The tears blinded her as she ran unheeding through wet grass chilling her ankles. Her wild rush over wet ground began to force her heart into greater effort and her breath came in shuddering gulps. Several times she stumbled and when she found a friendly old chestnut tree in her path, she sank down against it, too exhausted to go any further.

And there, crouched against the stalwart trunk, she laid her head against it and broke into bitter sobbing. Drops of rain caught by the thick foliage of the leaves plopped down on the ground around her as though the tree in weeping with her was trying to encourage her to wash away with her tears all the unhappiness of the past year.

She wept for Maura, for Maura's mother, for her own efforts of revenge, for the tragedy of Beau and his parents and for ... Armand, whom she loved better than anyone else in the world. When she stopped crying at last from sheer exhaustion, she lay with swollen eyes closed for a long time, and thought of poor Mistral. Then, as though the spirit of Mistral was answering, the thunder began to roll and lightning flashed. The natural action for self-preservation brought Sara to her feet stiffly and she moved lethargically from the danger of damp earth. Heavy drops of rain splashed upon her face and head as she left her shelter. She was exhausted and drenched to the skin with the small flame of courage burning eternally inside her almost quenched.

Not caring, she stumbled on through the mist of rain and lifting up her head wiped her face with a sodden handkerchief. Then, like a mirage in the desert of despair, there it was – the Petit Chateau. Suddenly, like a bird homing to its nest, Sara was running towards it, remembering the key always kept in a little niche by the entrance door in case of emergency.

And it was there Armand found her many weary hours later. After searching the Chateau he had toured the grounds on his horse without success and was returning home when he made a detour past the Petit Chateau. His keen eyes soon pinpointed the key left in the door and with fresh hope in his heart he swung from his mount, tethered it to a tree and walked in. One by one he strode through all the rooms, and even his strong heart began to quail when each door was opened to reveal an unoccupied room.

There was only the nursery left – the last place he expected to find her in. And there she was, sitting on the floor fast asleep with her head against his old rocking horse. He closed the door quietly behind him and leaned against it. The relief he felt on seeing her there made him feel strangely weak. He remembered how he had sweated as he rode past the swollen river thinking she might have met with an accident, struck her head and fallen into the strong current to be carried away.

With a smothered exclamation of relief, he just stood there looking at her. The room was filled with shadows through which her pale gold head gleamed. Armand folded his arms and his mouth lifted into a smile, incongruously endearing, which had Sara seen it would have sent her heart rocketing. Her face was half hidden and as he moved closer to her across the room he could see the tear stains down one cheek. He also saw that her even breathing was racked at intervals by dry sobs and his face went grim.

As he bent down she stirred uneasily as if aware of his presence, then slowly opened her red swollen lids. Moments passed as she emerged from the realms of a deep exhausted sleep to focus on his dark, intent face.

He touched her flushed cheek caressingly with the back of his hand. 'Sara,' he said urgently and huskily.

For a while she was too beaten and upset to speak until with the quick perception of love she noted his tired, half reproachful look. That was how it would always be, she told herself wildly – reproach on his part, self-reproach on hers. Rolling over quickly out of his reach, she sprang to her feet.

'No, don't touch me! I'm going back to London.' Her voice rose in panic as at each backward step she took Armand took one forward. 'Don't touch me!'

Swiftly she backed across the room until she reached the wall to stand looking up at him palpitatingly as he reached her.

'Why should I not touch you, *ma petite?*' The black eyes gleamed and he seized her wrists to haul her into his arms. He held her so tightly that it was impossible for her to struggle. And he laughed, kissing her face, her swollen eyelids and tear-stained cheeks.

'Let me go!' she stormed. 'You will never forget the reason I married you. Can't you see how impossible our marriage is?' Once started, she could not stem the bitter flow of words. She had found part relief in tears and the rest had to come with words. Her pent-up feelings were unleashed, Mistral's death and her part in it and Armand keeping silent when she had accused him of being involved in Maura's end, all came out incoherently.

'*Doucement, ma chère reine,*' he whispered against her ear, and used the most effective way of silencing her.

For a long time there was silence while his mouth, demanding yet gentle on her own, finally got the response he sought. Only when she stood unresisting in his arms did Armand release her lips to lay his firm cold cheek against her hot one.

'You foolish *enfant*. Do you think I could ever let you go after what has happened between us? I told you there will be no annulment. You are mine, and what I have I hold.'

'But you're not being fair,' she accused him.

He released her enough to glare down into her working face. 'Fair?' he echoed. 'Do you call it fair to ask me to give up the sun, moon and stars, and the very air I breathe? – because that is what you are to me.'

Sara closed her eyes and said piteously, 'Don't you see I ran away because I couldn't face you after I knew everything – how unjustly I had treated you and ... and the trouble I've brought you.'

There was a brief silence, and she opened her eyes to see him regarding her with a humorous though sad smile. There was a gleam in his dark eyes which made her heart race breathlessly.

He said quietly, 'And you thought I would hold it against you that you sought revenge for your friend? *Ma petite*, I love you all the more for being so blindly loyal. You took a course which you knew full well could mean the sacrifice of your own happiness. Yet you had to be quixotic about it.' He hugged her. 'What a wonderful wife you are going to be!'

Sara stared at him incredulously. 'You really mean that? You won't ever hold it against me about ... Mistral either? I ... I loved her too. I didn't know what I was doing that morning. You see, I had received a letter to say that Maura's mother had died practically of a broken heart. It was brought on through the loss of her beloved daughter.' Tears welled in her eyes. 'How I hated you that morning!'

'So you took off on the first horse available, which happened to be Mistral. She died in harness the way she would have chosen. If there was anything she loved it was riding in a storm. She was born during a violent thunderstorm and she knew no fear of them. Knowing Mistral, I would say she would be more concerned for your safety.' His eyes narrowed, for Sara had closed her eyes to shake her head despairingly. 'And now what?'

178

The eyelashes Sara lifted again were wet. 'Oh, Armand! Why didn't you tell me you were not the man in Maura's tragedy when I accused you on our wedding night? If you loved me surely you could have told me?'

'It was because I loved you so much that I kept silent. I knew you did not love me as I loved you and I did not want you any other way. You had to love me in spite of what you heard or believed about me. I wanted no fair weather love but a deep, lasting one. I will endeavour to explain – but first let us be comfortable. You are tired, *chérie*.'

Sara was indeed sagging against him, and lifting her into his arms he sat down with her in the big armchair which had belonged to his nannie. Then sitting her comfortably on his knee he drew her head against him and began.

'That first time I saw you across the swimming pool at the hotel I flicked you a glance I would give to any stranger. Then I found I could not take my eyes away from you. There was an untouched quality about you, a serenity of beauty the like of which I had not encountered before. I knew a strange thrill of excitement I had never felt for any woman. Here, I thought, is the woman I have been unconsciously searching for all my life but never expected to find. The next moment a man joined you and I cursed myself for being all kinds of a fool. Just my luck that I had found you too late! I was not to know that fate was on my side and was planning even then to push you into my arms that evening when we collided and I trod on your poor little foot. I was so sorry I had hurt you, and I felt your pain as my own.'

He gave her a kiss on the top of her head. 'Your attempts to freeze me off puzzled and intrigued me. It occurred to me that the man I had seen you with that afternoon at the pool meant nothing to you, because you seemed to be so unhappy. You wore no ring and I put it down to a broken love affair. I felt I could deal with that. But though I sent you flowers and forced my attentions upon you, I made no headway with you. There were moments on the ski-slopes when I felt we were getting closer, but they never lasted and by that time I had got to know you and was desperately in love with you. All I knew was I had to have you quickly, marry you first and woo you afterwards. We had all our lives in which to get to know each other. I was shattered when you told me on our wedding night that you had never loved me – that you had married me for revenge.'

Sara lifted her head and said pleadingly, 'I fought against loving you. If only you'd told me then that it was your cousin and not you as I'd thought.'

'I knew nothing about it. I was away when it happened and I came back to attend the funeral of my cousin's parents. I did hear at the British Embassy about your friend's tragic death, but I knew nothing of her association with my cousin.'

Sara said on a note of surprise, 'Then you never met Maura?'

'Never. Immediately after my cousin commenced work at the Embassy in Paris I was sent abroad on an important mission. In the meantime, your friend Maura came to work at the Embassy.' He pinched her cheek. 'I am still of the opinion that she died accidentally by taking her sleeping pill after consuming too much alcohol. It is happening all the time.'

Sara sighed. 'I wish I could be sure of that. I can't forget how distressed she was in her last letter to me. She was very much in love with your cousin and couldn't bear the thought of leaving him.'

'Then why leave him if she loved him so much?' Armand argued. 'She could have stayed on at the Embassy. They would only have been too pleased to keep her on permanently. I believe she was very popular with the Embassy staff and everyone was sorry to see her go. You see, *ma petite*, when you hurled those bitter accusations at me I began making a few inquiries. It seems you have also. Who told you who Maura's boy-friend was?'

'Your cousin Beau.'

He looked startled. 'Beau? Is he home?'

'Didn't your mother tell you? He came to dinner.'

'No, When I arrived earlier, I had a quick word with

Papa, then dashed up to see you. I was aching to see you again. You will never know how I felt when you weren't there. I never want to go through the past few hours again wondering what had happened to you. Maman thought you had gone for a ride on Mimi before dinner, but I knew different because your riding clothes were still in the wardrobe.' He paused to control his voice which was less steady than usual. Then, 'Go on, tell me about it.'

Sara told him everything that had passed between herself and Beau.

'I told him nothing about us . . . I mean. . . .' she stammered on, crimson with embarrassment beneath the steady regard of his dark intent gaze. 'He has no idea I confused him with you. But what he had told me only confirmed my opinion that Maura had killed herself. You see, she was not a drinker apart from an odd glass of sherry or champagne when the occasion merited. I can only conclude that when Beau didn't arrive for her farewell party she drowned her sorrows in drink. Later, on returning to her flat, she could easily have made up her mind to end it all by taking the sleeping pills, knowing it would be fatal.'

Armand drew her head against his shoulder. 'Why not stop torturing yourself, *chérie*, by giving her the benefit of the doubt? Letters can be very misleading at times. By the way, talking of letters, I ached to get in touch with you while I was away, but it was impossible. All the weary time I was away from you I found myself bitterly resenting my job for the first time. I was aching to get back to you to begin our honeymoon in earnest after all the frustration of being parted. There will be no more partings, *ma chère reine*. I have resigned from the Quai d'Orsay, which was no easy task. They were bitterly opposed to it. But I was adamant.' The charming smile flashed with a hint of devilry in the black eyes. 'I want to be a father to my children, not just a name. I want to watch them grow and be with you when you need me.' He laughed, bending his head to rub his hard cheek against her flushed one. 'That was some blush, *chérie*.

Now forget your poor little friend and concentrate upon me.'

Sara lifted eyes filled with tears. 'Such a terrible waste of life – Maura, her mother and Beau's parents. Terrible for him to know he killed his mother and father.'

Armand looked stern. 'I will not have you torturing yourself over Beau. He is not worth it. To begin with, he lied to you. He would never have married Maura, or anyone else. He is not mature enough for marriage. He was ruined from birth by doting parents who pampered him and gave in to his every whim. You see, his mother had no children for ten years and could never resign herself to the fact that she might never have any. I believe she was terribly jealous when I was born and she doted on me. I was six when her son was born and she called him Armand after me.'

'He's not very fond of you. He's jealous.'

'He has little reason to be. I was prepared to love him like a brother. Like him, I was a lonely little chap, being an only son, and I welcomed him like a brother. But it was impossible to get near him. He was completely spoiled.'

'Then he must miss his parents dreadfully. How terrible to have their death on his conscience!'

Armand said grimly, 'Beau has been killing his parents for years with worry over his way of life. When he left university, he was supposed to help his father to look after the estate. But it bored him and he was never at home. He had an apartment in Paris and got in with a wild crowd. His parents were forever paying his debts to keep him out of trouble and he made a thorough nuisance of himself. I tried to get him interested in sport, but he was a bad loser and consequently created many embarrassing situations. As a last resort I persuaded him to apply for a vacancy at the Quai d'Orsay where he could work his way up into a really good position. He was accepted. Unfortunately, I was unable to help him settle in his job. I was sent abroad. Then, as I said about your little friend Maura, old habits die hard. Soon, I believe, he was back with the old crowd, drinking and gambling. This was the situation when

Maura arrived to work at the British Embassy. The rest you know. When I returned to Paris it was all over. I had obtained special leave for the funeral of Beau's parents. His mother was my father's only sister and her death was a great blow to him.'

Sara shook her head. 'I don't know what to say.'

'I am sorry to have to tell you this, but it was essential for you to know the facts. It all came out at the inquest on Beau's parents, his dismissal from the Embassy and the fact that he had been drinking heavily before taking his parents out in the car. Incidentally, they were not on their way to Paris as Beau would have you believe. They were on their way to dine with my parents. Beau overshot the entrance of the Chateau and crashed into a tree.'

She stared at his dark intent face, shattered at Beau's lying. 'Was he charged with dangerous driving?'

'Yes. But my father procured the services of an eminent counsel and Beau escaped with a heavy fine providing he went voluntarily to a place for alcoholics to be cured of his drinking.'

Sara looked up into his face, drawn slightly with re-membered pain. He would have been very fond of Beau's mother and would have been as shattered as his father at her sudden death. Life had not been easy for him either this past year. He could be blaming himself that he had not been available at a time when he could have helped Beau most with his job. And there had been the anxiety over his father's health and her own bitter revenge had not helped. Tenderly, Sara framed his face in her hands. 'Thank you for telling me about Beau and for putting my mind at rest about Maura.' Her lips were warm and fragrant on his. 'I love you so much, Armand. I realized how much each day you were away,' she assured him as she drew away.

He turned his mouth into the palms of her hands as they framed his face.

'I know you do. Yet there are still shadows in these blue eyes, and I know what is causing them.' His smile was tender. 'We are going to be married again, in church this time. Before I came home I called in a dress salon in Paris where a fashion show was in progress and picked your wedding dress. The model wearing it was a similar build to you. It is cut on classical lines in white Brussels lace, and I am sure you will adore it.'

'Armand,' Sara breathed ecstatically with stars in her eyes. 'Oh, Armand! How lovely! When ... where?'

'This week-end in the little village church where my parents were married. In the meantime, do not forget we are already married.' He was smiling, but a tiny flame flicked in the depths of his black eyes, causing her to drop her eyes in confusion.

For something to say, Sara teased, 'So you were gallivanting around Paris looking at beautiful models while I was pining for you!'

'You shall pay for that untimely remark later,' he said darkly.

She had to kiss him then. He tasted the salt of her happy tears and all the sweetness beneath. And she clung closer with her slim body fierce and loving, her arms tight around his neck. Ardent minutes passed and the shadow deepened around them.

Much later Sara asked about Beau. 'What is going to happen to Beau? I must know because Maura loved him so much.'

'We shall work something out when he comes home for good.' He glanced at his wrist watch. 'Mon dieu! My parents will be wondering where we are. We have probably missed dinner.'

Instantly, Sara was all wifely concern. 'Poor Armand! I expect you're ravenous. When did you last eat?'

'Not since breakfast. I was in a hurry to get back to you.'

Sara rode back to the Chateau seated in front of Armand on his horse. And held safely in his arms she found the peace which had eluded her since Maura's tragic death was hers for all time.

They were married in the pretty village church, old grey, ivy-covered with its graceful Norman tower and solid walls built to defy centuries of weather. It was a sunny morning with all the estate workers and villagers turning out in their Sunday best to wish them well. All of them, right down to the six demure little French girls who were her bridesmaids, thought what a vision of loveliness she was in her lace wedding dress.

Radiantly, she walked into the church on the arm of Claude Ravel, who had come down expressly to give her away. And on that short journey down the aisle to where Armand stood waiting for her Sara was dimly aware of the sun slanting rainbow torch like beams through the stained glass windows on to masses of roses, lilies, mimosa, violets and primroses beautifully arranged around the church.

After the ceremony they were driven from the church along cobbled streets between half-timbered houses with curved fronts and quaint leaning upper stories gay with window boxes of flowers. The church bells rang out joyously, following them along lanes between green pasture land and wheat fields. Around a bend in the road they came across two Sisters in the flowing robes and stiff white winged headdress of their Order sitting in wait for them on a farm gate. They waved joyously, almost losing their balance as they craned forward to see the bride.

Lausanne shone like a jewel in the sun when Armand and Sara arrived at their palatial hotel overlooking the lake on the first stage of their honeymoon. Nearby was a park and beautiful gardens ablaze with flowers leading down to the lake. Brightly painted streamers rubbed against small boats on the water and the crystal clear air appeared to dance like a mirage before the eyes.

Armand and Sara had dined in the hotel where they had been waited on by a courteous staff eager to please. Sara had never in her wildest dreams imagined that life could hold so much happiness. It shone in her blue eyes, in the enchanting oval of her face with its healthy natural bloom of a ripened peach and in her sweetly curving mouth. Armand belonged to her for all time, with no brooding looks back over her shoulder at the past.

After dinner, they had gone for a sail on the lake and

had strolled back to the hotel through beautiful grounds where green lawns reminded Sara of Penhurst Towers and Maura. But her memories of her friend were no longer bitter. They were poignantly sweet and tucked away in the past where they belonged. She was beginning a new life centred on Armand and the Petit Chateau to which they were going to return after their honeymoon.

With a smile of pure happiness, Sara pictured herself riding with Armand, crooning softly to her infant son – peeping into the kitchen of the Petit Chateau for a word with the cook and slipping across to her neighbour the Comtesse for her valued advice. Heavenly thoughts, heavenly world, she mused, leaning back contentedly against Armand's broad chest as they stood at their windows before going to bed. The view was breathtaking and Sara sighed with utter bliss.

'Happy, *chérie*?' Armand whispered in her ear as he breathed in the sweet fragrance of her hair.

Sara turned her face to him. 'So happy that I wish time would stand still at this very moment.'

'Why now?' he murmured against her mouth. 'If time has to stand still let it be when we are in bed. What could be more ecstatic?'

And as usual he was right.

# THE OMNIBUS
## Is Here!

## A GREAT NEW IDEA
# From HARLEQUIN

# OMNIBUS — The 3 in 1 HARLEQUIN
only $1.50 per volume

Here is a great new exciting idea from Harlequin.
THREE GREAT ROMANCES — complete and
unabridged — BY THE SAME AUTHOR — in one
deluxe paperback volume — for the unbelievably
low price of only $1.50 per volume.

To introduce the Omnibus we have chosen some of the
finest works of four world-famous authors . . . .

> JEAN S. MacLEOD
> ELEANOR FARNES
> ESSIE SUMMERS
> MARY BURCHELL

. . . . and reprinted them in the 3 in 1 Omnibus.
Almost 600 pages of pure entertainment for just
$1.50 each. A TRULY "JUMBO" READ!

The first four Harlequin Omnibus volumes are now
available. The following pages list the exciting
novels by each author.

Climb aboard the Harlequin Omnibus now! The
coupon below is provided for your convenience in
ordering.

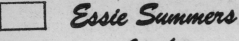

# Essie Summers
## Omnibus

Miss Summers once said that she could fill a book with words she loves. Perhaps this is the main reason why her many thousands of readers have come to know, that when her fingers touch on typewriter keys — the most enchanting characters spring into life.

.......... CONTAINING

BRIDE IN FLIGHT ... begins on the eve of Kirsty's wedding to Gilbert when the phone call arrived that was to shatter her life. Kirsty's immediate instinct was to run, blindly away, back to New Zealand, her childhood home, and this led to even more complications. (#933).

MEET ON MY GROUND . . . introduces Sarah Macdonald, secretary to Alastair Campbell. To Alastair, they were perfectly matched, but Sarah had a mental block where Alastair's money and position were concerned, which Alastair worked very hard to remove. (#1326).

POSTSCRIPT TO YESTERDAY . . . tells of how thrilled Nicola Trenton was when her distant cousin George Westerfield invited her to New Zealand to share in the local Centennial celebrations. But Forbes Westerfield was against her coming from the start, and he made his feelings so perfectly clear. (#1119).

$1.50 per volume

# Jean S. Macleod
## Omnibus

An author who has endeared many thousands of readers with her books wherein she frequently uses a background of her birthplace, the west coast of Scotland. The authenticity with which she writes of the breathtaking lochs and mountains, captures and takes the reader with her as the story, in its beauty, unfolds.

. . . . . . . . . . CONTAINING

THE WOLF OF HEIMRA . . . Introduces young Fenella and her love of the Hebridean island of Heimra. Her fiance, Val, the new-found heir to the island laird, and Andrew MacKail, with his bitter resentment of them both. (#990).

SUMMER ISLAND . . . set on the lovely Loch Arden, to where Ailsa MacKay returned when her mother became ill. Perhaps the old romance between Ailsa and Gavin Chisholm might have blossomed again, but there had been too many changes at Loch Arden. (#1314).

SLAVE OF THE WIND . . . takes us with Lesley Gair to Glendhu, where the dark mountain peaks of Wester Ross loomed above the glen. She was mistress of the family estates now, and this stranger, Maxwell Croy was intent on buying back the part which had once belonged to his family! (#1339).

$1.50 per volume

# *Eleanor Farnes*
## *Omnibus*

A persuasive and most appealing author with an insatiable appetite for travel. Miss Farnes' ability to re-create and share the charm and beauty of vivid locales and spellbinding characters has rewarded her with an abundant following of avid readers.

.......... CONTAINING

**THE RED CLIFFS** . . . a charming story, centering on a delightful Devonshire cottage. Alison lived and worked in London, and had no particular interest in the old cottage, left to her on her brother's death. That is — until the overbearing Neil Edgerton laid claim on the place! (#1335).

**THE FLIGHT OF THE SWAN** . . . the story of young Philippa Northen's release from a mid-Victorian upbringing. Her happiness to find at last, the attentions of an attractive man surrounding her. And then, the threat of jealousy from another woman, which could destroy everything for her! (#1280).

**SISTER OF THE HOUSEMASTER** . . . tells of Ingrid Southbrook, who came to keep house at a boys' public school, set in a pleasant old cathedral town. Her meeting with Patrick Southbrook, whom she expected to be selfish and disagreeable, and her surprise to find him quite, quite different! (#975).

$1.50 per volume

# *Mary Burchell*
## *Omnibus*

An exciting writer, with an adventurous appeal, who discovered her flair for writing romance at an early age. Her true to life characters and the vivid locations come alive, as she weaves the unmistakable Mary Burchell books, which have captivated an abundant following of avid readers.

. . . . . . . . . . CONTAINING

A HOME FOR JOY . . . is offered so kindly, by her uncle and aunt, upon the sudden death of her father. Joy was more than grateful to them, but in the end they were to benefit as much from Joy as she had from them! (#1330).

WARD OF LUCIFER . . . tells of the struggle between Norma, who knew from the beginning what she wanted, and of Justin, who used her only to further his own interests. When would Justin come to the realization that Norma's happiness was the most important interest in his life! (#1165).

THE BROKEN WING . . . a touching story of Tessa Morley, crippled, and her bewitching twin Tania, who had always had everything. Would she now win the love of the temperamental Quentin Otway, to whom success seemed the only thing that really mattered. (#1100).

$1.50 per volume